Love is
a time of enchantment:
in it all days are fair and all fields
green. Youth is blest by it,
old age made benign: the eyes of love see
roses blooming in December,
and sunshine through rain. Verily
is the time of true-love
a time of enchantment—and
Oh! how eager is woman
to be bewitched!

ISLAND LEGACY

Annabelle Todd had an excellent reason for bidding way beyond her means for a Cavendish painting. But the autocratic man who outbid her must have wanted the portrait very badly to have paid so much more than it was worth. Whatever was he up to? Annabelle resolved to get the picture back to its rightful owner—but how?

KAREN EDMUNDS

ISLAND LEGACY

Complete and Unabridged

ULVERSCROFT
Leicester

First published in Great Britain in 1985 by
IPC Magazines Ltd.,
London

First Large Print Edition
published May 1990

British Library CIP Data

Edmunds, Karen
  Island legacy.—Large print ed.—
  Ulverscroft large print series: romance
  I. Title
  823′.914[F]

  ISBN 0-7089-2203-1

Published by
F. A. Thorpe (Publishing) Ltd.
Anstey, Leicestershire
Set by Rowland Phototypesetting Ltd.
Bury St. Edmunds, Suffolk
Printed and bound in Great Britain by
T. J. Press (Padstow) Ltd., Padstow, Cornwall

1

"THE bid is against you, madam."

Anabelle Todd remained very still, her clear grey eyes fixed firmly ahead. Her opponent was somewhere in the front row. He—or she—was not using a catalogue to indicate bids as Anabelle did. A more subtle technique had been employed, by a more experienced adversary.

Silence fell suddenly over the scattered audience gathered under canvas. Seated on serried ranks of red velvet and gilt chairs, elegant couples ceased their low murmurings and turned their attentions to the auctioneer. From the corner of her eye, Anabelle saw several of them crane their necks in an attempt to identify the bidders. She knew the painting had already reached a price way above its reserve and, surely, way above its value to anyone else but her? Anabelle's heart began to beat faster in panic. She *must* have it.

The quietly authoritative voice of the

auctioneer droned on. "Fifteen two, fifteen two. An original Cavendish. At fifteen thousand two hundred pounds."

Anabelle's elbow clutched more tightly at the black leather bag tucked beneath her arm. The banker's draft, securely zipped into the change pocket, carried a maximum of fifteen thousand pounds. She groaned inwardly. Connolly's, the sale agents, had assured her the portrait would go for about ten thousand pounds, twelve at the outside. She thought she had allowed a good enough margin.

The auctioneer's keen eyes swept the interior of the marquee. "Are you all finished, ladies and gentlemen?" He paused. "At fifteen thousand two hundred pounds to the gentleman in the front." He paused again before adding clearly, "Once."

Anabelle chewed on her lip. There was extra cash at home, she knew. But it was earmarked for the bookshop and flat. Joanna, her mother, wanted to buy the freehold for their future security. And, Anabelle also knew, Joanna Todd desperately wanted to buy back the portrait. She

2

gazed at the painting, at the familiar serene face in its ornate gilded frame.

"Fifteen thousand two hundred pounds —twice."

Her features froze. It had gone very quiet. The atmosphere was oppressive; warm and humid. Then her arm moved. The catalogue twitched. She was just in time.

The auctioneer's reactions were precise; practised and speedy. "Fifteen four," he snapped.

Anabelle concentrated on the front row. She watched carefully. A dark masculine head turned very slowly to one side, giving her a clear view of its lean angular profile. He had unruly black hair which curled over the collar of a navy blue blazer. His skin was lightly tanned and he had a square jutting jaw and a long straight nose. Equally slowly he turned back. Anabelle continued to stare and saw a slight movement of his dark head, an almost imperceptible nod.

"Fifteen six." The auctioneer's eyes glinted with excitement.

Catalogue pages rustled as the small

audience began to seek information and whisper. Anabelle knew by heart what was written there: *LOT 36 "JO" by Paul Cavendish. The untimely death of this talented young artist in the prime of his career has made his paintings particularly rare and collectable.*

She had to buy the portrait now, before its value soared beyond their means. The conversation buzzed around her. Anabelle clenched her teeth and raised her right arm more boldly, flicking the stiff white catalogue defiantly.

"Fifteen eight."

She'd find the money. She'd get it from somewhere, anywhere. She must have that portrait.

"Sixteen thousand. Sixteen two. Sixteen four." The auctioneer's head moved rhythmically from side to side taking each bid in turn. His expression was impassive.

Anabelle's heart began to thump uncontrollably. Her mouth became dry. She leaned forward, grasping the gilt back of the empty chair in front of her. A thick curtain of light golden hair fell across her face, obscuring her vision. Pushing it away

4

impatiently, she continued to bid as if in a dream.

Seventeen thousand.

Eighteen thousand.

She hesitated for a moment, thinking frantically, 'I must be going mad. I can't possibly afford this. '

The black head turned fully round at exactly the same second as her catalogue moved again.

"Eighteen two."

Anabelle found herself looking at a pair of narrowed deep-set eyes, their colour obscured by thick dark lashes. Straight black eyebrows were drawn together in a frown and his lips set into a cold hard line. Lean cheeks emphasised his angular features. His eyes remained steadfastly on her as he gave, again, a very slight nod.

"Eighteen four."

With determination, Anabelle controlled her breathing, inhaling deeply and slowly as she lifted her chin marginally to show her defiance. She bid again. Outwardly confident, she was inwardly quaking. It had never occurred to her that someone else would be as interested as she in the portrait; interested enough to pay way above the going rate for an oil painting of an unknown woman—even if it was a Cavendish.

Who was he, this dark stranger? Why should he want a portrait of an ordinary Englishwoman from a very ordinary background unless . . . For an instant, the idea that he might be a Cavendish flashed across her mind. But immediately she dismissed the thought. From what Joanna had told her, the Cavendishes were fair-haired and fair-skinned and typically British in appearance. This man looked definitely foreign, and a bit of a rogue to boot, she realised! What if the portrait went out of the country? Galvanised into action, she continued to bid.

Nineteen thousand.

Twenty thousand. *Twenty thousand?*

Anabelle inhaled sharply. This was crazy. That kind of money was beyond her —and Joanna. They would never be able to raise it. The reality of this fact exploded in her head causing her cheeks to flush with emotion. Tears pricked the back of her eyelids. She was unwilling to accept that she was defeated, that the picture was slipping from her grasp.

"Twenty thousand." The auctioneer swung his attention to Anabelle. There was silence. His voice hardened marginally as he queried, "Madam?"

There were many pairs of eyes on her. She swallowed and shook her head emphatically. Her shoulders sagged as she looked down ruefully at the red jute carpet beneath her black court shoes. Anabelle listened to the now familiar procedure of the lot being offered again to the audience in general—without success. It seemed that no one could match the price the dark-haired man was prepared to pay.

Crack! The gavel descended indicating completion of the sale. With a satisfied expression, the auctioneer addressed the buyer. "Your name, sir?"

A rich deep voice answered, "Dalgetti. Mark Dalgetti."

Dalgetti? Anabelle frowned. He sounded foreign. She guessed she was right. The portrait would be exported.

Depressed, Anabelle rose to leave. There was no point in staying any longer. She had come only for the painting. Her adversary stood up at the same time.

Hesitating, she fingered the back of the ornate gilded chair in front of her. He turned fully to face her.

Anabelle had dressed carefully that morning, as she always did. When she was at work in the bookshop, she liked to look neat and unobtrusive; presentable but not too outstanding. There had never been a great deal of money for clothes, so that good service rather than trendy fashion was her maxim.

She often chose the classics because they didn't date and, although she liked many fashionable styles, she wore only those that suited her and ignored the rest. Today, her simply-cut, grey flannel suit was brightened by a pretty white blouse with frills at the neck and cuffs. It gave her a cool efficient appearance which, at that precise moment, belied her inner turmoil.

Mark Dalgetti stared at her. His eyes travelled lazily over her flushed countenance taking in every inch of her discomfort. Anabelle straightened her shoulders. She tossed her head back and flicked back her long silky hair to challenge his gaze.

But he did not flinch and she could only

retaliate by lifting her chin to show that she didn't care. Hateful man! He knew she would have to walk down the aisle, right past him in order to leave. Was he going to stare at her all day?

She glared back. He was tall and attractive, she noticed grudgingly, with an arrogant set to his broad shoulders. Underneath his navy jacket, he wore a soft white cotton shirt and well-cut trousers. At his throat, not a tie or cravat as Anabelle might have expected, but just a glimpse of lightly tanned skin. It gave him a wild rakish appearance which complemented the black untamed hair, yet was at variance with his stylish clothes.

The auctioneer announced a break for lunch and people began to drift away. Anabelle seized her chance and fell in behind a flamboyant couple who effectively shielded her from view. But as she walked past the front row, she was aware that his eyes remained on her and burned uncomfortably into her back until she escaped into the sunshine.

After morning rain, the weather had brightened and the air smelled fresh, but it did nothing to alleviate Anabelle's sense of disappointment. She chewed on her lip and wondered if it was worth approaching this man Dalgetti and explaining. If he was a dealer there might still be room for negotiation. Paintings were just property to some collectors.

She sighed heavily, realising how upset her mother would be that she had failed. She wouldn't show it, of course, though they both knew that Joanna had especially wanted *this* Cavendish. And why not? Anabelle thought defiantly. Joanna had more right to it than anyone else. It was, after all, a portrait of herself.

Anabelle loitered indecisively on the freshly-raked gravel drive between the long low stable block and the grassy paddock that served as a car park. A germ of an idea had formed in her mind. Joanna already had another Cavendish painting. She had come across it years ago, quite by chance, and scraped together the money to buy it. It was a later one, painted shortly before Paul Cavendish died. The later ones, some critics said, were better. If she offered this dealer another Cavendish instead of the portrait, would he be interested? she wondered. She decided it was worth a try. She lingered in the shade of an old walnut tree and waited.

As the minutes ticked by, she became increasingly apprehensive that she had missed him, although she knew he would have to come this way to the car park.

The crunch of gravel made her jump. Mark Dalgetti came swiftly round the corner of the stables, tucking a bulky wallet into the inside pocket of his blazer. He did not have the portrait with him. Presumably, because of its size, he had arranged for it to be sent on. He drew level with her and, for a second, her courage failed. She stayed in the shadow of the tree as he continued past her, striding purposefully towards the car park.

"Mr. Dalgetti!" She almost shouted his name.

He stopped abruptly and spun round on his heel. "Yes," he said shortly.

Anabelle stepped tentatively from the shade.

"Oh, it's you," he added.

They stood in silence for a few awkward moments and looked at each other. Anabelle realised it was up to her to continue. She saw his straight black eyebrows draw together in a frown as his gaze intensified. The keen glitter of his narrowed deep-set eyes threw her off guard and her rehearsed speech seemed to vaporise into thin air.

"What do you want?" he asked pointedly.

There was just a trace of foreign accent in his speech. Nothing much; only a hint in the way he said 'want'. Italian? she guessed. His name and appearance suggested so. She gathered her thoughts hurriedly but, before she could speak, he became impatient.

"Is something bothering you, Miss—er?" He raised his eyebrows in query.

"Todd. Anabelle Todd," she muttered, stalling a little.

"Well, Miss Todd, what is it?" he returned sharply.

She took a deep breath and tried to look taller than her five feet four inches would allow. "Mr. Dalgetti, do you really want the portrait?" she began.

His mouth twisted in disparagement. "That's an odd kind of question to ask a man who has just paid twenty thousand pounds for it."

"I mean, does it have to be that one? Wouldn't another one do?"

"No, another one would *not* do," he replied grimly. "If that were the case, I should hardly have paid twice the market value for it, should I?"

There was more than a hint of sarcasm in his voice and Anabelle's confidence waned. She fingered the clasp of her handbag. Through her clothes she felt the heat of the sun on her back.

"But why that one?" she pressed. "What does it mean to you?"

He heaved a sigh of thinly veiled exasperation. "Miss Todd, that is none of your business and—"

"Yes, it is," she broke in impulsively, "you see . . ." She stopped abruptly as she realised it might not be wise to lay all her cards on the table just yet.

He waited for her to continue, then looked at his watch significantly. "I have an important meeting in less than an hour," he said briskly. "If you have something to say, would you kindly get to the point?"

Anabelle tried to speak slowly, but the words rushed out. "The woman in the portrait—do you know who she is?"

His expression changed immediately to one of guarded interest. He stepped towards her, regarding her shrewdly. His eyes, Anabelle noticed with surprise, were not brown, they were green; a clear intense green, glinting like cold glass.

"Do you?" he asked slowly.

"Yes."

"And are you going to tell me, Miss Todd?"

"I might," she hedged.

The contempt on his face told her instantly that this was quite the wrong thing to say. Mark Dalgetti was not a man to tolerate indecision. Obviously, he was a man of forthright action.

"You are wasting time," he retaliated acidly. "And, while yours may not be valuable—" he paused—"mine is. I believe there is nothing further for us to discuss."

"No, wait," Anabelle answered quickly. "I want that portrait. Name your price, Mr. Dalgetti." She didn't stop to think of the consequences of her offer, but she needn't have worried.

He gave her an impatient humourless laugh. "It's not for sale. You've lost, Miss Todd. Accept the fact."

"No." Her protest came hoarsely, yet audibly, like a stage whisper. Her hands clenched tightly and her eyes flashed in defiance.

He had half-turned to leave. The passion in her voice must have penetrated even his calculating persona, for he stopped and turned back. Again his keen eyes searched her face as they had done earlier in the marquee.

"Who are you?" he demanded.

Anabelle's mind raced. If she told him, she would have played her hand and she would have to rely on his good nature to appreciate her claim to the portrait. And if he had no good nature? She held her breath. She had already told him to name his price.

Before she could reply, he took a step towards her and lifted the curtain of light silky hair that obscured part of her face. His brief touch on her skin sent an unexpected tingle down her spine. Instinctively, Anabelle jerked her head backwards, but his strong hand entwined in her thick hair and gripped firmly so that she cried out in pain.

Her head tipped and her hair fell behind her shoulders, fully revealing her features. His face was near to hers as he surveyed her closely.

"I noticed earlier your resemblance to the woman in the portrait," he went on. "It's mainly around the eyes. Who are you, Anabelle Todd?"

His physical nearness overwhelmed her. He was tall, and powerfully built. To resist his hold on her would be futile. But, at least, now she knew why he had stared at her. She glared at him in retaliation and snapped, "You're hurting me!"

He released her and, as he drew away his hand, he allowed his fingers to travel slowly through her hair so that the silky fronds floated gently into place, brushing coolly against her skin. Anabelle's body reacted involuntarily to this sensuous movement and she shivered.

She recovered quickly. "Thank you," she said curtly, tossing her head. She increased the distance between them pointedly, though, she realised, there was no sense in hedging from the issue further. She raised her chin proudly and said clearly, "The woman in the painting is Joanna Todd, my mother and—" she hesitated and swallowed—"the artist, Paul Cavendish, was my father."

She waited for his reaction. He was startled initially, then his expression changed to one of suspicion.

"He doesn't believe me!" she thought. She pressed on speedily with her case. "So you see, Mr. Dalgetti, we—Joanna and I —do have a special interest in the portrait. If you particularly want a Cavendish painting, then we have another, better one. Perhaps we could arrange an exchange?" she suggested. "With some cash adjustment?"

His expression was impassive apart from a tiny movement in his eyes as they darted over her. It was as though her words had fallen on deaf ears. Undaunted, she went on briskly, "May we come to some agreement, Mr. Dalgetti?"

He replied after a long silence in which Anabelle, though she hadn't realised it

17

until he spoke, had been holding her breath.

"Where can I contact you, Miss Todd?"

She exhaled and her heart leapt. Inwardly, she felt triumphant.

"I'll give you my card," she answered, extracting one from her bag. It was her business card for the bookshop that she helped her mother to run. Her home had the same address as they lived over the shop.

He looked at it, read it, then tapped it rhythmically against his fingernails.

"And where might I contact you, Mr. Dalgetti?" Anabelle prompted.

He ignored her question and continued as if by way of explanation, "I know very little of the relative merits of Paul Cavendish paintings, or his—" he stopped as though he'd had second thoughts. "If it's true what you say about your relationship—"

"Of course, it's true!" she interrupted.

"Then why—" He paused again. His mouth twisted in speculation. "The portrait isn't mine to barter. I'm simply acting as an agent for the man who wants to buy it. He wasn't well enough to make the journey to England."

Anabelle's heart sank. She had been right. The painting would be leaving the country. "May I ask where your client lives?" she ventured tentatively. It was a bit of a cheek, she realised, and he probably wouldn't tell her, but it was worth a try. Therefore she was surprised when he answered.

"Italy," he said, watching her closely again.

"Oh."

"The island of Ischia, to be precise." A slight frown furrowed his brow. His eyes narrowed. "In the Bay of Naples. Do you know it?"

She shook her head. She'd heard of Capri in the Bay of Naples, but not Ischia. She sensed he didn't approve of her reply. "I see," he said.

"See what?" she thought.

Again, he tapped her card on his fingernails. "I'll inform my client of your offer." For the first time, a smile etched across his well-shaped mouth.

"Thank you." Anabelle offered her

hand. "I look forward to hearing from you, or your client."

They shook hands and he gave her an acknowledging bow, before wheeling around to walk swiftly away.

Anabelle was left puzzled. She still had a chance for the portrait, she was still in the game. Yet, she had a distinct impression that Mark Dalgetti was playing according to different rules. He had been so cool, so controlled throughout the auction and their subsequent conversation. And yet, he had been startled by her revelation, she was sure.

Why hadn't she had the presence of mind to ask him more questions about his client or—her confusion turned to doubt —about Mark Dalgetti himself? Anabelle walked slowly along the path. Her shoes crunched on the gravel. She wondered whether it had been wise to give him her card so easily. After all, what did she know about him? Nothing. Absolutely nothing.

Anabelle felt exhausted by the time she had driven home to the shop in Lanchester. She was emotionally drained by her experience and paused to compose herself before opening the door into The Bookstack.

Joanna was talking to their senior assistant at the till. She looked expectantly at Anabelle. Anabelle bit her lip, frowned and shook her head. Her mother's face fell, though she straightened the cardigan jacket of her oatmeal knitted suit and squared her shoulders in a philosophical shrug that was typical of her.

Anabelle tried to smile, but she knew how much her mother wanted the portrait. Her wish for the painting was not for reasons of vanity, though, if it were a true likeness, Joanna must have been a very beautiful girl twenty years ago. Anabelle looked at her now. The good bone structure and unusual violet-blue eyes were still there, but the years had taken their toll of her skin and hair. Lines of worry across her brow and greying hair were indications of the struggle Joanna had had in bringing up a child on her own and running a business at the same time.

She's only forty, Anabelle thought, and made a mental note to book Joanna a day at their local hairdressing salon and beauty parlour as a surprise birthday present.

They were very close and Anabelle valued her good relationship with her mother. It was more like having an older sister sometimes. She could see Joanna's disappointment behind her brave façade and it tore at her own heart.

"Shall we eat out tonight, Mum?" Anabelle suggested brightly.

Joanna shook her head. "I'm rather tired, dear."

"I'll pop round the corner for a bottle of wine then?"

Joanna smiled and nodded, and Anabelle retraced her steps to the street outside. She'd save the news that all was not lost until later.

The Bookstack was in a Georgian terrace close to the centre of Lanchester and just off the main thoroughfare. The shopping centre was pedestrianised and that made their particular lane a relatively quiet corner. It was a pleasant place to work and live.

In the wine merchants, she was wandering around the shelves, looking for something a bit special, when a familiar voice interrupted her train of thought.

"Well, if it isn't sexy little Anabelle!"

An arm slid round her shoulders and she was stifled in a bear hug.

"Roger!" she reproved, pushing him away firmly. "Do behave yourself!"

Roger Mason had been friendly with her since schooldays, when he had tormented her by pulling her pigtails in the playground. That made it all the more difficult for her to fend off his constant advances. As a casual acquaintance, she liked him well enough and he was fun to be with. But, on a more personal level, she found him altogether too familiar. In their teens they had often attended the same parties and dances, and Roger had invariably held her too close for comfort on the dance floor. Any kisses she had allowed had always been too heavy and too lingering, and she had been quite relieved when he had gone away to university so that she didn't have to risk offending him with her constant refusals.

"You're looking very smart today, Anabelle," he said. "I must say, such cool elegance really does something to me."

"Stop it, Roger," she chided, half-laughing to hide her mild discomfort.

"There's a Young Farmer's Rally on

Saturday," he went on, unperturbed. "Are you going?"

"I can't. I'm working," she replied, glad of a ready-made excuse.

"How about the barbecue in the evening? Come with me in my new sports car."

"I'd love to go." She smiled. "But I'm afraid I'm busy."

Roger looked petulant for a moment. "Got somebody else lined up?" he muttered moodily. "Anyone I know?" He shoved his hands roughly into his pockets.

Anabelle hurriedly reached for a bottle of rosé from the shelf. "I'm sorry, Roger, but I've got to rush. Thanks for asking me, all the same."

She escaped as quickly as she could. She'd lied about being busy on Saturday evening. She shrugged. A Young Farmer's barbecue would have been fun—but not with Roger Mason.

Anabelle had known him for almost as long as she had lived in Lanchester. Joanna had moved from London eighteen years ago when Anabelle was a small child. She'd taken on the run-down bookshop and had worked hard to build it into a going concern as Anabelle grew up.

Anabelle wasn't particularly academic at school. She preferred the creative crafts—sketching, painting, needlework and even cooking when there was something special to do. When she was old enough, she applied her creative flair to the shop layout as well as their flat. Anabelle's natural inclinations complemented Joanna's who, perforce, was more concerned with turnover, profit and loss.

There had been mistakes in the business, Anabelle knew. Joanna had learned many things the hard way and frequently sought professional advice.

One or two of these advisors had occasionally taken more than a professional interest in Joanna's affairs. A beautiful widow with her own business had seemed a powerful attraction. There were proposals of marriage, but Joanna turned them down and Anabelle began to realise that Joanna was still very much in love with the memory of her father. It must have been a cruel blow when he was tragically killed.

Anabelle was too young at the time to

recall what had happened. Joanna always avoided talking about the accident and its repercussions on their life since. But Anabelle knew it was tied up with the reason that, despite Joanna's love for her husband, she had ceased to use his name and reverted to calling herself by her maiden name of Todd.

2

" **J**OANNA wants that portrait more than anything," Anabelle reflected wistfully as she walked back to the bookshop. It was the one thing, Joanna had told her, that she and Paul regretted selling when they were younger. But they had to eat and there was baby Anabelle to think of. Paul had promised Joanna he would buy it back "when they were rich". It was never to be, for he didn't live long enough. "After he died," Joanna had said, "I promised myself that, if I ever had the capital, I'd do my utmost to buy it—for his memory. It was his favourite."

"And now we have the capital," Anabelle thought angrily, "someone else comes along with more. It's just not fair!"

It was strange, she mused, how everything seemed to happen at once. Joanna had struggled for years with The Bookstack, and now it was a success and paying well, they suddenly found themselves the recipients of a substantial legacy in the form of a house.

Joanna was the only child of elderly parents. They hadn't wanted her and had farmed her out to boarding school as soon as they could. It wasn't only children that Joanna's parents didn't like, they hated all noise as well; planes, the new by-pass, pop music, anything. They were oppressive to live with and Joanna had found a flat in London straight after school. They didn't object when she wanted to marry, although only seventeen, and they had been even less interested in their grand-daughter, Anabelle, who had arrived less than a year later.

But blood is thicker than water. Mr. and Mrs. Todd had died recently within six months of each other and left everything to Joanna and Anabelle. So now, although not exactly rich, they had access to capital. Joanna took up her quest for the portrait, and began negotiating for the freehold of the shop and flat. For the first time in their lives they felt really secure.

Joanna traced the portrait through two galleries to a private collection. Anabelle had been quite prepared to go to the owners, state their case and ask to buy it outright. The news of the auction forestalled that, but Anabelle was sure no one else would want it as much as they did. She had been confident of success. So had Joanna. Anabelle waited until the last customers had gone and they had closed the shop before relating the incidents at the sale.

"Twenty thousand?" Joanna was astounded.

"I didn't dare bid any more."

"I should think not! Where would you have got that amount from? I wonder."

"Well, I thought—I mean—" Anabelle chewed her lip. "There's Grandma's Will, isn't there?"

"You know that's spoken for." Joanna spread her arms. "For here."

"But you'd rather have the portrait, Mother," Anabelle returned quickly. "Wouldn't you? Admit it!"

Joanna smiled and nodded. "Yes, I would. And I also have your future to think of."

"Well, I'd rather have the portrait as well," Anabelle retaliated valiantly.

"That's no excuse for recklessness,

dear," Joanna rebuked gently. "Come on, let's start dinner."

Their flat had a separate entrance from the shop and they climbed the stairs to the two floors above. Over the years, Joanna had furnished it, where possible, in keeping with the Georgian period of the property. Most of the furniture was reproduction, but there were one or two genuine pieces which had been picked up in sales and lovingly restored—mainly by Anabelle.

The Paul Cavendish painting that they owned hung on the wall of the first floor landing that was their hall. Joanna had found it quite by chance several years ago in a local art gallery and had scraped together the money to buy it. It was a futuristic composition of young people enjoying themselves at a party. The faces were very expressive and there was a touch of surrealism about it which Anabelle found disturbing, though visitors whose opinion she respected remarked how good it was.

It reminded Anabelle of the offer she had made to Mark Dalgetti. As they walked by it, she said lightly, "Would you rather have the portrait than that one, Mother?"

"Well, that's really one of my favourites, but I'd never sell it, darling."

"No, I mean, if it came to a choice, say, between the two. The portrait or that one?"

"The portrait, of course. It's always been extra special to me. Why do you ask?"

Anabelle told her of the offer as they went into the kitchen.

"I didn't realise you'd actually spoken to the man who bought it," Joanna commented. "What was he like?"

"Awful," Anabelle responded instantly. "Impatient, overbearing and—"

"What did he look like?" Joanna had stopped what she was doing and was frowning.

"He was big. Tall, I mean, not fat. With black hair—" she paused, thinking—"and the most intense green eyes I've ever seen." The memory of them came back to her so vividly that she blinked and swallowed. "Foreign, I imagine," she added.

Joanna seemed relieved. "You're sure? Not English?"

"I don't think so. His name's Dalgetti. He—he didn't give me his card." She bit her lip. "I gave him mine though."

"Anabelle! That was a foolish thing to do!"

"I know! I had no choice! I didn't want to lose the painting and he was only acting as an agent for someone else."

"An agent? For whom? Did he say for whom?"

"No. He just said he'd pass on my offer."

Joanna was staring into space. "I was wondering who else would want to pay so much for one of Paul's works," she said quietly.

"The auctioneer said that Paul Cavendish paintings were becoming collectors' items."

But Joanna was shaking her head, "Whoever bought that portrait wanted it for similar reasons to ours. Personal ones."

"What?" Anabelle demanded incredulously. Who but they would want it? Then she realised. "Oh. You mean one of the Cavendish family?"

The Cavendish family. A taboo subject. Anabelle knew her father had been alienated from his family before he married her mother. And she also knew that Joanna avoided talking about them. It was something to do with the accident and it still pained her to this day.

"Mark Dalgetti said the man who wanted the portrait lived on Ischia, Mother," Anabelle added.

Joanna sat down and rubbed her temples with her hands.

"Why should the Cavendish family be interested in Father's paintings? You said they disowned him. You said—"

"Please, darling," Joanna broke in. "I'd rather not talk about it. I'll just say this. Rupert Cavendish, your grandfather, has lived on Ischia for the past ten years." She looked up. "It's too much of a coincidence, isn't it? He must be involved somehow. Though why he should want a portrait of me—even if it was painted by Paul—I have no idea. He hated me. He blamed me for everything." Joanna sighed heavily. "We might as well forget all about the painting now."

Anabelle felt her anger rising. Mark Dalgetti must have simply been playing

33

her along! No wonder he had smiled at her. He must have pitied her naïvety and had never had any intentions of seriously passing on her offer. She wished now that she'd bid even more at the auction and made him pay forty thousand for the portrait.

The rift between Joanna and her father-in-law was deep. Whatever had happened in the past still pained Joanna, and Anabelle was reluctant to ask. One day, she thought, they'd discuss it; when the time was right.

That day was precipitated on them sooner than Anabelle expected.

Anabelle was scrambling eggs in the sunny kitchen when Joanna came through with the post.

"The usual," she muttered, leafing through the circulars and invoices. "Oh— and one from the estate agents in London." Joanna had been thinking of expanding the business with another shop and was viewing possible properties.

"Any for me?" Anabelle called over her shoulder.

Joanna didn't reply. Anabelle stopped stirring and turned out the gas. "The eggs are just ready," she said cheerfully. "Hungry, Mum?" Then she noticed Joanna's face.

She had gone quite pale. The letters were dropped on the breakfast table, except for one which was held between her slightly shaking fingers.

"What is it, Mother?"

"It's for you," Joanna replied. "Airmail. From Italy." She handed the letter to Anabelle. "You'd better read it right away. It's from him—your grandfather. I'll finish the toast."

Anabelle took the envelope and sat down. Her name and address were hand-written; flamboyant, flowing script in black ink, not Biro. She took out the folded sheet of paper and read.

Joanna placed the scrambled eggs on toast in front of her and remarked, "It is from him, isn't it? I recognised his writing. To be honest, I've been expecting this since you came back from the auction."

That was three weeks ago, Anabelle thought. She had assumed it was all over and forgotten, but clearly Joanna had not.

"Rupert wouldn't let an opportunity like

that—" Joanna stopped abruptly as though she had said too much.

Anabelle re-read the letter. It was a simple presentation of facts. He was Rupert Cavendish, her grandfather and, perhaps, she knew very little about him. He understood she wanted a portrait painted by her father, his late son. He was prepared to make her a gift of the painting if she would travel to Ischia to collect it, and remain as his guest for a few weeks. It sounded very formal to Anabelle. She looked again at the address. It was a hotel address in Ischia.

"He wants to *give* me the portrait, Mother."

"In return for what, I wonder?" Joanna murmured.

"Mother! You sound cynical."

"Maybe I am," she replied crisply. "But Rupert Cavendish never did anything without a selfish motive in the past and I've no reason to believe he's changed. Your eggs are getting cold, dear."

Anabelle fell silent. Joanna wasn't cynical or vindictive by nature. She must have good reason for her attitude towards Rupert Cavendish. Anabelle put down her knife and fork and, leaning forward, asked baldly, "Mother, what happened? Why do you hate him so much?"

Joanna heaved a sigh and pushed aside her plate. "Rupert had fixed adeas about life. He was a patriarch and what he said was law. He tried to manipulate your father's life, then mine, and then," she hesitated, "after the accident, your life as well. You did what Rupert said, or else."

"Or else—what?" Anabelle prompted.

"Oh, he used all kinds of pressures; financial, emotional. He wanted Paul to join a merchant bank in the City, but Paul wanted to paint. As Rupert became more autocratic, Paul became more rebellious until, eventually, he left home. Paul went to live in London and, shortly afterwards, he met me and we fell in love. Rupert was convinced I was at the root of the trouble and that I was only after Paul's money." Joanna laughed drily. "Truly, I had no idea Paul came from a wealthy family until Rupert tried to buy me off."

"Buy you off? So that you wouldn't marry Father?"

Joanna nodded. "Rupert offered me a

very large sum of money to go away and forget your father. I refused, of course. He threatened to disinherit Paul. Paul told him to go right ahead, and he did." Joanna shrugged. "Paul and I, and then you, simply went our own way, much to Rupert's chagrin.

"I—we—" Joanna began, but the memory was obviously painful. "It's all so long ago now. Perhaps Rupert has mellowed over the years. And he is your grandfather." She looked frankly at her daughter. "If you wish to go and visit him, I shan't object."

"What are you saying, Mother? That maybe you and Father were wrong? That you regret your actions?"

"Not at all. I'm saying, I suppose, you have the right to decide for yourself about your own grandfather."

"Come with me," Anabelle suggested.

"No."

"Why not?"

"I can't." Joanna shook her head. "I once swore to Rupert's face that I never wanted to see him again, and I meant it." She laughed quite harshly. "Not that it bothered him except—except that I had you and he wanted you. That's what all this is about, you see, darling. You."

"Me? How? Why?"

"You're a Cavendish. Whatever your name, you have Cavendish blood in your veins. Aren't you curious? Don't you want to visit him?"

"Not without you."

"I'm not invited."

"That's no reason, Mother," Anabelle exploded, "and you know it! There's more to it, isn't there? What haven't you told me? Why should he extend an olive branch to me and not to you?"

"I doubt it's an olive branch, darling. More like an inducement. You could have been brought up a Cavendish, Anabelle. Wealth, position, nannies, good schools, even the right husband would have been picked out for you, I expect." Joanna swallowed. "After your father was killed, all those things were offered."

"By Rupert Cavendish?"

"By your grandfather, if—" Joanna stopped.

"If what?"

"If he could be your legal guardian. The papers were drawn up while I was recovering from the injuries I sustained in the accident. Rupert wanted me to give you up; to sign away my rights as a mother. I refused. I refused you a life of luxury because I thought that the love I could give was more important than any amount of money." Anabelle noticed the gleam of a tear in her mother's eye as she concluded. "Was that wrong of me?"

Anabelle was shaking her head. "Never. No, it wasn't the wrong thing to do. A man who could even think of such a thing is a monster."

"Not a monster, darling. Autocratic, possessive, possibly vengeful to a certain extent. He never forgave me for marrying Paul and taking him—and you—away from him. I expect he still wants his pound of flesh. Make no mistake, Anabelle, he wants you back in the family fold as a Cavendish."

Anabelle made a great show of screwing up the letter and tossing it from hand to hand. "Then I shall be delighted to thwart his plans. Rupert Cavendish can keep his bribing gifts. And his precious family name. I'd rather be a Todd any day."

Suddenly, a thought crossed her mind. "I'm sorry. Mum. It means we lose all hope of getting the portrait."

Joanna shrugged her shoulders philosophically. "We can't have everything and I fear the price might have turned out to be too high."

"I agree," Anabelle added firmly. She aimed the screwed-up letter at the waste-paper basket.

"Aren't you going to reply at all, Anabelle?" Joanna asked with a slight frown.

"No. I have better things to do. Come on, we'll be late opening the shop."

It was too late for reconciliation now, Anabelle reasoned. Why, if she hadn't given her card to Mark Dalgetti at the auction, Rupert Cavendish wouldn't even know where to find her. She wondered if Mark Dalgetti had traded the information on that card. It wouldn't surprise her. He'd looked the sort. An opportunist, she decided. Too clever by half. His lean tanned features immediately sprang to her mind. She could recall them vividly; the wild dark hair and the watchful eyes.

Irritated, she pushed thoughts of him away and got on wiih her work.

Joanna's letter from the estate agents in London was more promising. Within the next few weeks she viewed several properties—none of them suitable—and became fired with enthusiasm for the new venture.

Anabelle stayed behind to run the shop. She enjoyed coping with The Bookstack in Joanna's absence. They employed competent, trustworthy staff and it was a pleasant task.

On one such afternoon, Anabelle was tidying up before closing. Joanna had been in London all day. She had taken an early train and was staying up in town for dinner and a show with a friend.

The shop was quiet. There were one or two browsers engrossed in paperbacks. Anabelle had given their senior assistant a couple of hours off to do some shopping, leaving herself the job of checking the till and locking up.

Her evening was planned. She was going to wash her hair, make an omelette and then finish off the cream silk négligée set she was making for Joanna's birthday. It was almost complete. She had already been up to the flat during the lunch break to lay out the slippery silk. It had been a nightmare to sew on the machine and she was stitching on the rich lace trim by hand.

The last customer bought a paperback and left. Anabelle returned to tidying the bookcases and shelves. She cursed under her breath as she reached for the top shelf. If only it were a little lower—or she a shade taller—she'd be able to reach the books untidily strewn on top. Her low heeled sandals didn't help. She'd have to fetch the stepstool from the stockroom. Damn! She heard the shop door open. Another customer. She stretched and felt her checked cotton shirt part company from her camel cord skirt. She jumped. Her fingers brushed the spine of the offending book. One more try, she thought. Just a bit higher! She flexed her knees to give more momentum to her spring.

Then suddenly she was moving effort-lessly upwards towards the book, and her hand closed around it. Someone had lifted her! Someone strong, for she was held comfortably aloft for several seconds.

She suppressed an annoyed gasp. "Roger Mason again, I'll bet," she thought irritably. "I must say something to him this time. Taking liberties like this in the shop is definitely not the same as pulling pigtails!"

"Roger," she began, hastily tucking her shirt back into her waistband. "Oh!" It wasn't Roger. It was Mark Dalgetti.

"Good afternoon, Miss Todd." He reached over her head and retrieved another wayward book for her.

"Thank you," she said stiffly.

"My pleasure, I assure you," came the smooth reply.

The same shrewd green eyes, the same hint of foreign accent. What was he doing here? Anabelle resisted the temptation to ask him outright and consequently could think of nothing else to say. She stood there stupidly, dumbly realising how inadequate she must seem.

He looked more relaxed than at the auction. There was an easy smile on his well-shaped lips. But still, she noticed, a question in his piercing eyes. He wore a fine grey wool sweater beneath his jacket and a pair of black cords. She supposed he was waiting for her to say something.

"Good afternoon, Mr. Dalgetti," she said woodenly. "What can I do for you?"

His straight black brows shot up. "Now there's an invitation for any man!"

Anabelle compressed her lips and studied the spine of the book in her hands. "I'm rather busy," she said pointedly, and turned to replace the book on the shelves.

"I want to buy a book."

She inhaled slowly and faced him again. She could hardly refuse to serve him. "Do you know the name of the author?" she asked politely.

"No," he replied.

"The title?"

"'Fraid not."

"You're not being very helpful." She paused slightly and then added, "Sir."

"I know the topic of the book," he volunteered.

"Which is?"

"'How to handle prickly booksellers'."

Anabelle clenched her fists and counted to ten. She took a deep breath, looked him straight in the eye and said, "Get to the point of your visit, Mr. Dalgetti."

He responded immediately. "Rupert Cavendish is concerned about you. You haven't replied to his letter."

"I think his concern is a little late in the day, don't you?"

"Maybe," he conceded. "But I understand your mother's behaviour left him no option."

"It was his—" she began heatedly, then stopped. Whatever her views, they were no business of Mark Dalgetti's. She tried a different tack. "Did you pass on the offer I made for the portrait?" She suspected he hadn't. Perhaps he was here to try and buy *their* Cavendish as well as the portrait.

He didn't answer her. He looked around the empty shop and asked, "Is Joanna Todd here?"

"Not at the moment."

"But you did receive the letter?"

"I did."

"May I ask why you chose not to reply?"

She reflected on the way he had avoided answering her earlier question and thought "sauce for the goose". "You may." She smiled sweetly and added silently, "But I shan't answer." "Now, if you'll excuse me, Mr. Dalgetti, we're just about to close."

She walked away, ostensibly carrying on with her work. She knew he was watching her, but when he loomed up beside her at the till, she feigned surprise. "Oh, are you still here?" she remarked.

He placed a large glossy hardback on the counter, and said, "I'll take this one, please."

Damn him, she thought, pursing her lips, would he never leave? She picked up the book and checked the price. It was an expensive, technical one on Naval architecture. The Bookstack carried a good selection of nautical books. Lanchester was near to the coast and there was a large marina at Lanstead, a few miles away. It provided a steady demand for any text connected with the sea. She slipped the book into one of their distinctive paper bags with its logo of an untidy pile of books.

He paid cash, using two crisp twenty pound notes which looked fresh from the bank. She handed him the parcel with his change, avoiding his eyes. He unsettled her. She knew he wasn't going to go away and she wasn't sure what she could do about it. What did he want from her?

"Thank you," he murmured, pocketing the change. "I'd like to talk to you, Miss Todd, if we can arrange a mutually convenient time." He raised his straight black eyebrows as he looked at her, "Shall we say dinner, tonight?"

"I'm busy this evening and, frankly, I don't think we have much to say to each other. When I made my offer at the auction, I had no idea you were working for Rupert Cavendish. My mother guessed at the truth when I told her the painting was going to Ischia. Now I know the background, whatever you have to say, I'm afraid I don't want to know."

"But you do want the portrait?" he rejoined smoothly.

No. Yes. No. The words bounced like ping-pong balls in her head. Yes, of course she did, but at what price? She remained silent.

"Well?" he pressed.

"I've made my offer," she said stiffly.

"Oh, come now, Miss Todd!" His tone was derisory. "A wealthy old man doesn't *sell* a portrait painted by his only son to his only grandchild."

"What?" she uttered without thinking. She didn't know she was his only grandchild. Her father had had a sister, hadn't he? A sister called Eleanor.

Mark Dalgetti must have noticed her hesitation at this news, for he followed up his implied criticism of her behaviour with, "We can't discuss it here. Have dinner with me at my hotel tonight."

"No." Perhaps he did have something important to say. Surely it wouldn't take long? "No, thank you," she added hastily. "I've told you, I'm busy this evening." She looked at her watch. "It's past closing time and I have to lock up."

"I'll take you home," he suggested.

"I live here. Over the shop," she explained patiently.

He smiled crookedly. "I know."

She glanced at him sharply. What else did he know? she wondered. She sighed. He wasn't going to leave without saying what was on his mind. "All right," she agreed. "You'd better come up. I'll make some tea."

"Is your mother home?" he asked as she hung up his jacket and placed the wrapped book on the hall table.

"Not yet," she said.

"All alone? Do you usually run the shop alone?" He sounded surprised and that annoyed her.

"I'm perfectly capable, Mr. Dalgetti, of dealing with any problems that might arise." Except perhaps this one, she thought. His tall spare frame seemed to fill the hall. The arrogant shoulders looked powerful. She went on hurriedly, "Actually, my mother's in London on business, though I'm expecting her home any minute now."

He didn't appear interested. His attention was taken by the Paul Cavendish painting on the wall. "Is this the one you offered in exchange?" he enquired.

"Yes," she answered levelly. "Technically, it's a good one. Better than the portrait, I'm told and, I presume, more valuable."

"That's a matter of opinion." He shrugged. "The value of anything is simply the price one person is prepared to pay. If someone else wants to pay more,

50

well—" he spread his hands to emphasise the point—"isn't that what happened at the auction?"

Anabelle frowned. She didn't like the value of her father's work reduced to monetary terms only. "Value isn't always measured in hard cash," she argued fiercely. "Some of us find other things more important."

"Such as?" He seemed vaguely amused by the notion.

"Happiness, freedom, love," she retaliated sharply. "I don't suppose you or Rupert Cavendish would understand the meaning of those values."

He drew in his breath and his eyes narrowed. "Ouch," he said softly. Then she felt awful for behaving rudely.

"We're getting away from the point." She sighed wearily. She waved her arm at the painting. "Please feel free to examine it while I make the tea."

As she laid the tray, she wished she had a silver one with a Georgian teapot to match to impress him; so that he could go back to Rupert and report that she and Joanna were doing very nicely, thank you.

But she hadn't and they had to make do with an ordinary tea-service.

The tray was heavy as she'd put on the remains of a jam sponge and some plates as well as the tea. He took it from her in the hall. She was glad to be relieved of the weight, yet, at the same time, she wished he hadn't. She showed him into the living-room with ambivalent feelings.

She realised too late that the cream silk and lace sewing was spread out for all to see on their mahogany dining-table. Mark Dalgetti noticed it immediately. His glance lingered appreciatively. With no embarrassment at all, she thought sourly. Any decent man would have looked away.

"Er—over here, please," Anabelle directed, indicating the coffee-table in front of the fireplace.

Anabelle felt her colour rise as she caught him studying her again, and she didn't like it. She turned her attention to pouring the tea.

This is a mistake, she fumed silently, clattering the cups and saucers. I shouldn't have asked him here. It's too late now.

He's here. I'd better find out why and send him on his way.

She handed him a cup of tea. "Did you pass on my offer, Mr. Dalgetti? I'm sure as an art dealer you'll appreciate it was a generous one."

"I'm not an art dealer. What gave you that idea?"

"You said at the auction you were acting as an agent."

"I also said I knew very little about Paul Cavendish paintings. Even less about Joanna and Anabelle Todd—or should it be Cavendish?" He paused. "Of course, I'm better informed now." He regarded her seriously.

She asked him again, "Why are you here, Mr. Dalgetti?"

"To take you back to Ischia, to visit your grandfather."

His directness stalled her for a moment, but she soon recovered. "And if I don't want to go?" she queried archly.

"I'll persuade you."

"How?" She laughed harshly. "By strong arm tactics? Yes, it wouldn't surprise me. You look as if you're not above breaking the law when it suits you.

Don't bother, it'll be a waste of effort. You can take a horse to water, but you can't make him drink!"

"I have no intention of using force," he flung back tightly. "And your grandfather has no intention of allowing you to buy the portrait. As far as that's concerned it's already yours."

"I don't want it."

"That's a lie! You're too proud to accept it, you mean!" he challenged.

"But it isn't offered unconditionally, is it? He wants me to go out there and collect it. That's not a gift. It's a bribe." Her voice had risen and the colour heightened in her cheeks. She had been sitting by the coffee-table to pour the tea. Now, she stood up and moved across the room to gaze out of the window and compose herself.

She heard him put down his cup and saucer. "The hatred runs very deep, doesn't it?" he said.

"He caused a great deal of un-happiness."

"And maybe he's sorry," Mark Dalgetti snapped. His tone was edged with anger as though he was losing patience with her.

"It's too late," she replied bitterly.

"Yes, he was afraid of that."

She swung round to face him and leaned against the window ledge. "If he's so anxious about me, why does he send you —one of his heavies? Why doesn't he come himself?"

Mark Dalgetti rose to his feet and strode across the room to confront her. He was angry, she could see. His lips were compressed into a thin line and his breathing was rapid. "He's an old man," he seethed through clenched teeth. "His health isn't good."

"So why should I care?" she retaliated. Anabelle didn't recognise herself. Why was she saying these things? She *did* care. Of course she cared that her grandfather was ill.

He took her by the arms, pushing his fingers into her skin, and shook her soundly. His green eyes flashed ominously. "Because he's your grandfather, you stubborn woman!" he ground out.

She glared at him, her grey eyes wide with defiance. She glared first at his tightly controlled expression and then at each hand in turn as he continued to grip her arms. Then, with all the coolness she could muster, she said, "And I owe allegiance to my lord, I suppose? Those days are gone, Mr. Dalgetti. Now, would you please let go of my arms? You're hurting me."

It seemed a long, long time before he did.

He gave a short dry laugh as he dropped his hands and stepped back. "Huh! I thought I was going to enjoy this job. How wrong can you get? A trip to England, an attractive woman—yes, Miss Todd, I had noticed your personal attributes. You're attractive all right, but you're also hard— too hard for my liking."

No! She wanted to deny it. It wasn't true! He only knew half of the story, Rupert's half. And he was out of the same mould as Rupert, believing that women should do as they're told. Anabelle studied the floor. Her comfortable sandals were dusty from a day in the shop. They looked shabby beside Mark Dalgetti's well-polished black leather shoes. His were probably hand-stitched too. She wondered how much he was being paid for this "job" as he had called it.

She lifted her head. "My mother wasn't included in the invitation. Do you know why?"

"Rupert Cavendish refuses to talk about her."

"Then don't you understand my position? I can't possibly be disloyal to her."

"He sees her as the woman who took his only son from him," he countered evenly.

Anabelle shook her head. "That's not true. The rift was there before he met my mother. My father hated him."

Mark Dalgetti sighed impatiently. "Hate. Bitterness. Is that all I am to hear from you? Have you stopped to think why your grandfather wants to meet you now? After all those years of silence? He's an old man. And you won't even give him a chance."

She pushed her fingers raggedly through her hair. "I don't know what to think," she muttered finally.

He seemed to sympathise, but she couldn't tell for sure. Sometimes his expression was unfathomable. He walked briskly to the telephone-table and scribbled something on the pad.

"The invitation still stands, Miss Todd. I have a yacht and crew standing by in Lanstead Marina. We plan to leave for Ischia next week, hopefully with you on board. Of course, I realise you'll want to talk it over with your mother. When you've reached a decision you can contact me at the Lanstead Manor Hotel. The number is on the pad." He stopped to draw breath and, as he did so, his shrewd eyes passed quickly over her, taking in every single detail she was sure. Nothing would miss his attention.

He continued. "Think carefully about what I have said. This is only the first step." He gave her a brief acknowledging bow and moved to the door. "Thank you for the tea. I can find my own way out."

She was left staring at the half-empty cups, uncomfortably aware that the aura of his presence remained behind in the room to haunt her.

3

ANABELLE finished the silk and lace négligée with mounting tension. She refused to let her agitation upset her progress, and managed to gift-wrap the present carefully and hide it in her wardrobe before her irritation erupted.

Emotional blackmail, that's what it was! How dare he? He had implied her grandfather was sorry about the past. His words still echoed round the empty room. "He's an old man. His health isn't good". Damn Mark Dalgetti! Of course those sentiments got through to her. She couldn't ignore them. If her grandfather genuinely grieved for her affection, she could never forgive herself for not responding. Yet, supposing it was a ploy? To deliberately come between Anabelle and Joanna, and effect some kind of retribution for the past?

Incensed by the idea, she ripped the top sheet off the phone pad, screwed it up and threw it in the bin. Joanna had said she would be home very late. The evening dragged, and Anabelle felt bewildered and rather miserable.

She went to bed early and slept heavily at first, only to wake suddenly in the middle of the night. After that she dreamt dislocated dreams of herself standing inside a circle and trying to face all directions at the same time until she was dizzy.

The next morning her mother woke her with a cup of tea.

"You look flushed, dear," Joanna said, "and I heard you mumbling in the night. Are you feeling ill?"

"No, I'm fine." She yawned. She felt exhausted. "I didn't sleep very well."

"You were sound asleep when I came in. I peeped in to say good night."

"Did you have a good day in London?" Anabelle smiled as she pushed herself into a sitting position.

"I enjoyed my trip, thanks," Joanna replied. Then she grimaced. "Shop rents are sky-high in London. I'm going off the idea."

"We don't need another shop to survive, do we?"

"No, but you've shown such promise in

helping to run this one, I thought a shop of your own would let you spread your wings."

"I can do that here." Anabelle smiled.

"Then you can retire."

"I don't want to retire, thank you." Joanna grinned.

Anabelle leaned back against the pillows in comfort. "All right. I'll be the one to retire."

"No, you won't, young lady." Joanna flicked playfully at the counterpane. She smiled affectionately. "You're too useful. I'm proud of you, darling. You've turned out well, despite all our ups and downs."

A lump rose in Anabelle's throat. "Oh, Mum, you've never said that before."

"Well, don't let it go to your head. Don't forget I'm biased. How was yesterday in the shop?"

"One or two things cropped up."

Their conversation turned to business problems.

The more she put it off, the more difficult it became for Anabelle to mention the subject of Mark Dalgetti's visit. The mere fact that she'd invited him into the flat somehow seemed so disloyal. After a while she realised there was no sense in taking the risk of upsetting Joanna anyway. She had no intention of going to Ischia. Mark Dalgetti could go and jump in the sea for all she cared. Trips to the Mediterranean on yachts indeed! Heavens, that was a different world from hers, and one that she wanted nothing to do with. She was happy as she was.

In the event, it was Joanna who broached the subject, a few days later. They were sharing a cosy evening at home, dressed in jeans and sweatshirts, catching up on reading, writing letters and mending.

Suddenly, Joanna said, "Did you think any more about that letter?"

"Which letter?" Anabelle paused in her sewing.

"The one from Rupert Cavendish."

"You saw me throw it away." She shrugged.

"It's been on my mind. I wondered if it had been on yours also."

"Since you ask—yes. But I haven't changed my mind. I'm not going. I couldn't."

"Why not, dear?"

"Are you mad? After the way he treated you, and me, come to that, I'm not going to pander to his wishes—or those of his smarmy sidekick!"

"Anabelle! What on earth's come over you?"

"I don't know," she muttered irritably. "I'm angry, I suppose. I don't like being leaned on."

"No one's leaning on you, darling. I can't help feeling that what happened between your grandfather and me was a long time ago, and there's no reason why you should suffer because of it. It occurred to me he might have been trying to say so in his letter. An acknowledgement of—"

"Mother! What are you saying? I don't understand you," Anabelle interrupted.

"I'm not sure I understand myself." Joanna frowned and put down her book. "I was very young at the time, and impulsive. Your grandfather must be quite an old man now."

"Yes, he is." Anabelle saw Joanna's puzzled expression and continued with a helpless wave of her hands, "I wasn't going to mention it, but he came here to see me. Last week, when you were in London."

"Rupert came here?"

"No. The man who bought the portrait. Mark Dalgetti."

Anabelle told her briefly about the visit.

Joanna listened with increasing gravity and when Anabelle had finished said, "I think you should go."

"Why?"

"Because you are a Cavendish and I am not."

"You're beginning to sound like Mark Dalgetti, Mother. Whose side are you on?"

"The side of common sense. I know I've mellowed with age. I expect your grandfather has also."

Anabelle stood up, scattering her sewing. "All right, I'll go if it'll please you."

"Now, calm down, dear," Joanna soothed. "Don't you want to go? Aren't you even curious?"

Anabelle smiled ruefully, and sighed.

"Yes, I'm curious, and I admit I want the portrait. But I won't go without your blessing. I won't be used as a weapon against you. I love you too much for that."

"And I love you for your loyalty, Anabelle, darling. But you're proud and stubborn—as I once was. And as Rupert was. Perhaps he realises time is running out for him." Joanna was silent for a moment, then continued seriously, "I wouldn't compromise, you see. And neither would he. If your grandfather was prepared to believe such awful things of me, I wasn't going to be the one to enlighten him. That kind of attitude, unfortunately, can be a recipe for unhappiness."

"We've always been happy," Anabelle insisted fiercely.

"Yes." Joanna smiled suddenly. "You're a credit to me. Any parent would be pleased to have you as a daughter. I'd like your grandfather to know that, at least."

"Then he will," Anabelle resolved to herself. "I'll show him how well Joanna has brought me up without his money and interference. I won't have my mother misjudged so!"

"Do you want to meet your grandfather?" Joanna queried.

"Yes, I do."

"Then go, my darling. But tread carefully. I think we should have some more information from this Dalgetti man first."

Lanstead Manor Hotel was listed in the phone book.

Anabelle rang the next morning and they told her that a Mark Dalgetti was staying there, but was at the Marina all day.

She tried again in the evening and successfully got through.

"Yes. Dalgetti here," he barked down the line.

"This is Anabelle Todd."

There was a short silence. "Have you reached a decision, Miss Todd?"

"I'd like some more information first."

"Come and have dinner with me. You can ask as many questions as you like."

"All right," she agreed. "When?"

"Tomorrow. Here at my hotel. I'll send a taxi for you."

"That's quite unnecessary," she replied

crisply. "I have a car and I do drive. What time shall I arrive?"

They arranged a time and she rang off, wondering what she had let herself in for.

Lanstead Manor Hotel was an ornate Victorian building, internally modernised and set in extensive parkland. It was large enough to be used as a prestige conference centre and boasted a full size golf course in its immaculately kept grounds as well as convenient access to Lanstead Marina.

Anabelle parked her Mini Metro neatly between a Daimler and a BMW and walked across the tarmac to the imposing entrance. She'd borrowed one of Joanna's dresses for the occasion. It was a simple knee-length frock in delicate duck-egg blue silk with a deep scoop neckline edged by a matching flounce. It suited her colouring, giving a healthy bloom to her pale skin. She had piled her hair in a coil on the back of her head and left little wispy bits escaping round her face to soften the effect. Off-white shoes and bag and a woollen shawl completed her appearance. A few heads turned as she crossed the thick carpet to the reception desk.

The uniformed clerk, a pleasant-looking

young man, was expecting her. He came out from behind his desk with an appreciative smile and said, "Mr. Dalgetti sends his apologies. He was called away a few minutes ago to deal with an important telex message. Would you come this way, please?"

As they waited for the lift, he explained further. "I believe there's been some delay in his departure from the Marina. It's causing problems in Italy." He smiled at her as though he expected her to understand.

She was shown into a second floor suite.

"Will he be long?" she asked.

"I don't think so, madam. Can I get you a drink while you wait?"

"Thank you. A gin and tonic, please."

There was a small fridge and drinks cabinet in one corner of the luxurious sitting-room. Anabelle wandered over to the window while the clerk poured her a drink. The view was tremendous; over fairways, bunkers and copses to the distant sparkle of the sea.

"How lovely!" she exclaimed spontaneously.

"Yes, madam. All the suites on this side

of the hotel command the best views."
The clerk handed her a drink, and asked
solicitously, "Are you quite comfortable,
madam? Can I get you anything else?"

She declined and he left. But as he
opened the door, Mark Dalgetti walked in.

"I'm sorry, Miss Todd," he said
immediately. "I was called away unexpectedly."

He was so devastatingly attractive!
Anabelle blinked and swallowed. Dressed
in a dinner jacket and black tie he looked
almost respectable. Even his unruly hair,
though still long, was neatly combed. He
talked quietly to the clerk for a momen-
tand Anabelle saw a crisp banknote change
hands discreetly. He mixed himself a drink
and joined her by the window.

"I do apologise," he repeated. "An
unavoidable hassle, I'm afraid."

"That's all right," she muttered.
"Though I could have waited for you
downstairs."

"This is more private. It's very hectic
down there this evening. There's a conven-
tion due in."

"Oh, I see." She looked around the

69

sumptuous room. "He must be on a very good expense account from my grandfather to afford all this," she thought. Aloud she added, somewhat tetchily, "And it would be a shame to waste this beautiful suite, wouldn't it?"

He raised his eyebrows. "If you object to dining here, we can go downstairs. Have you any objections, Miss Todd?"

Yes, she had. Plenty. Was all this luxury to persuade her to go to Ischia? Or demonstrate the sort of life she'd missed? No, that sounded churlish. Perhaps it was Mark Dalgetti she objected to? That was more like it! He was just too damned confident for words. But she couldn't say that, so she shook her head and mumbled, "No, of course not."

She chose a chair and Mark Dalgetti sat opposite her on a sofa.

"Fire away, then. What do you want to know?"

She didn't know where to start. She was curious about her grandfather, and the rift between him and her parents. What kind of man disinherited his own son? Why did he hate her mother so much? And, more puzzling, why then buy a portrait of her?

70

She gulped down her drink and frowned into the empty glass. "Why now?" she began. "I don't understand why my grandfather waited so long."

Mark Dalgetti stood up and took her glass to refill it. "Pride," he stated. "You should understand that. You're like him in that respect."

"But the reasons for the rift are still the same. Nothing's changed."

"Yes, it has. You are an adult now. You have your own mind. And, as I've already said, he's old. His health is failing."

"Does he think all this will influence me?" She spread her arms indicating the luxury of the room, and saw his eyes narrow suspiciously as she took her second gin. "That's his strength, isn't it?" she went on tartly, "his wealth, this suite, the yacht, a home on Ischia." She paused to emphasise her final phrase. "Buying people off."

"Only those willing to be bought," he flung back swiftly.

"Like yourself?" she queried sweetly. "You seem to be enjoying the measure of his money."

Why did she say that? Why did Mark

71

Dalgetti bring out the very worst in her? She could see quite clearly she'd made him angry.

"I was thinking of you, actually," he said through clenched teeth. "And why you had changed your mind."

"Because of his money? I don't want any of his—"

There was a tap on the door.

"Dinner," Mark Dalgetti informed her. "I hope the idea that your grandfather might have paid for it doesn't make it choke you!"

There was a great deal of fuss. Several hotel staff brought in a mass of sparkling silver and glass, and pristine linen, laid neatly on trolleys. A table appeared and was set.

"Excuse me, Anabelle," Mark Dalgetti said, and moved away to talk to the man in charge.

Again, she saw bank notes discreetly change hands. The head waiter finished overseeing the display, checked the silver entrée dishes on their heated trays, then deftly withdrew the cork from a bottle of wine before slipping quietly from the room. They were alone again.

"Mr. Dalgetti—"

"Mark," he corrected. "It's easier."

"Why did you send the waiters away?" she asked.

"Do you really want a couple of strangers around while we talk?" he queried, surprised. "Does it worry you? Are you nervous of being alone with me?"

"Don't be ridiculous!" she retaliated, though he had voiced one of her doubts.

He came to stand squarely in front of her and his masculine presence was overpowering. He was so much taller than she, and so much broader. He carried himself well, straight backed, head high, yet he moved his limbs with supple grace and ease.

"I don't think it's ridiculous for a young woman to worry about dining alone with a man in his room," he said smoothly. "Especially a woman as beautiful as you are."

As he spoke, his encompassing green eyes swept over her. They took in everything; from the sheer stockings on her slim legs, to the delicate hollows of her collarbones. She wished suddenly that her shoulders and throat were not quite so exposed to his gaze, that her neckline was just a little higher. She had to resist the temptation to cross her hands over her neck and cover her nakedness, so intent was his inspection.

She raised her chin and replied firmly, "Don't worry about me. I can take care of myself. But I warn you, Mr. Mark Dalgetti, if you dare put a foot out of line, you'll answer to my grandfather. I'm sure you wouldn't like to lose your job."

"Well, at least we know where we stand." He shrugged. Then he grinned crookedly. "I gather from the remark that you've made up your mind to come to Ischia."

She hadn't meant to give her decision so early. She saw a gleam or triumph in his eye and responded, "All right, yes, I shall go to see my grandfather. Though whether I travel with you is another matter. I know nothing about you."

"And I know little about you. Shall we rectify that over dinner?" He took her hand and sighed impatiently. "Come on, Anabelle, a truce. A truce while we eat."

The meal was delicious—local oysters served on a bed of crushed ice followed by Chateaubriand fillet steaks and salads. They drank two kinds of wine, and Mark's behaviour was impeccable throughout. Her threat must have worked. Anabelle marvelled at how charming he could be when he tried. She asked about the yacht.

"The desk clerk mentioned a delay in your departure was causing problems. I hope it's not on my account."

He shrugged. "It's nothing serious." He grinned again and added, "A prize cargo is worth waiting for."

"He's nothing more than a bounty hunter," she thought. "He gets his fee when he delivers the goods." Aloud she said, "Don't alter your plans for me. I'm perfectly capable of travelling to Ischia under my own steam."

"The journey's much easier by sea," he responded. "Instead of taxis and trains, planes and ferries, you simply step aboard here and step ashore in Ischia. What could be simpler?"

"You're very persuasive. Are you in for an extra percentage, if you get me there in person?"

"Quite the little cynic, aren't you? If you're looking for a reason not to travel with me, I'll give you one." He topped up their wine glasses. "Yes, the desk clerk was right. Waiting for you to make up your mind has caused some problems. The skipper's had to return to Italy to rearrange the yacht's programme. We'll be short-handed and you'll have to pull your weight on board."

"Then count me out. I can tell you now, I'm no sailor. I'd be a hindrance."

"I wouldn't expect you to help sail her. She's a motor yacht, anyway, not a sailing one. I'm talking about day-to-day living, chipping in with the cooking and washing-up, keeping the boat tidy."

Anabelle glanced at the remnants of their sumptuous meal, and at the fruit savarin on the trolley that neither of them could manage. She wasn't able to resist a tiny little dig at the high standards he seemed to enjoy at someone else's expense. She waved her arms expansively and replied, "But I'm not in this league. I'm just a simple country girl. I couldn't possibly produce food like this." She struck home.

76

She was pleased to see that her deliberate coyness had irritated him.

He crumpled his napkin, threw it on the table and stood up. "All right, Anabelle, you've had your fun. When do we sail?"

"I haven't said I'm going with you yet."

His eyes glittered ominously as he leaned across the table towards her. "Don't play cat and mouse games with me, lady, or you'll be sorry," he threatened. "I'll order some coffee while you make your decision."

Just like that, she thought resentfully! He might be able to do exactly as he pleased, but she had other things to consider. She waited until he'd put the phone down, then said, "I've got to discuss it with my mother. We have a business to run and I can't leave her in the lurch. Besides," she finished grudgingly, "Joanna wants to meet you." Joanna had been firm about that. "Come to lunch on Sunday with us. We can make final arrangements there."

That seemed to placate him and he agreed. Anabelle stood up and began to search for her shawl and bag. "Good," she said. "Now that's settled, I'll be going.

Thank you for a delicious dinner, Mark."

"What!" He laughed incredulously. "You can't go now!"

"I don't see why not." She spied her bag on the sofa and walked towards it.

He moved swiftly to intercept her, but she darted round him. He was, however, too fast for her and *he* snatched her bag, holding it high above his head. Anabelle jumped to retrieve it and lost her balance. She would have fallen if he had not acted quickly to support her. A strong arm shot out and encircled her waist, but the other still held her bag away from her. Anabelle stretched unsuccessfully to reach it and for a few seconds there was a short ungainly struggle.

"How dare you?" she spluttered. "Give that back!"

He restrained her with ease, fending her off while he placed the bag on a nearby table and rummaged through it. Incensed by the invasion of her personal possessions, Anabelle's rage increased.

"What a despicable character you are," she seethed. "That's private property!"

But it seemed the more she agitated, the more controlled he became. He found what he sought. He withdrew her car keys, closed the bag, and handed it back to her.

"There," he said grimly, "you can go now."

Anabelle clutched it so tightly that her knuckles turned white. Who did he think he was, preventing her from leaving in this way? For the first time in her life, she knew what it felt like to want to hit someone very hard. Her heart thumped loudly in her throat.

"I insist that you return my keys immediately!" she flung out haughtily.

He rattled them in the palm of his hand. "If I do, what will you do?"

"After your behaviour just now, I think that's obvious!"

"I apologise if I was rough with you. You're a strong-willed girl and difficult to deflect from your chosen course of action." He hooked the key-ring around his index finger and extended his arm towards her. "OK. Take them. As soon as I see you get into your car, I'll phone the local police station. You'll be breathalysed before you reach the main road."

Damn him, she fumed inwardly. He was

right. She was bound to be over the limit after all that wine. Why hadn't she realised? What was wrong with her, for heaven's sake? She didn't usually drink at all if she had to drive! It seemed her common sense flew out of the window when Mark Dalgetti was around. She regarded the keys silently and chewed on her lip.

"They're safer with me," he concluded, tucking them into the pocket of his dinner jacket.

"Aren't you taking your mission a bit too seriously?" she challenged. "Though, on second thoughts, you wouldn't want to lose your percentage, would you? Do you get a bonus for delivering me intact to my grandfather?"

He was standing very close to her and his arm still rested, now lightly, round her waist. She was mesmerised by the glow in his eyes and she read danger in them.

"Bonus?" he queried softly. "Oh, yes, Anabelle, there's a bonus," he murmured, "but not in the way you think."

She felt as if she was being drawn towards him. Yet his hands on her waist barely touched her. For one crazy moment she thought he was going to kiss her. His face lowered to hers. Her chin came up, her neck stretched towards him. Then suddenly, his head jerked back and he was talking; not to her, but someone else—someone else who was at the door.

Anabelle hadn't heard the waiter knock, and that only increased her confusion. She must have been in a dream! She was almost in his arms and, what was more disturbing, she wasn't about to stop him! She would have let him kiss her!

Her heart thumped erratically. She tucked a stray lock of hair into her chignon. What *was* she thinking of? It must be the wine. Perhaps she'd imagined it? She looked at Mark. He was very composed, tipping the waiter, pouring the coffee. She must have imagined it. She accepted her cup of coffee gratefully.

After a second cup she felt better. Mark suggested some fresh air and she agreed. He kept his distance, she noticed, not touching her at all as he indicated the way and opened doors.

They strolled along the floodlit terrace outside the hotel dining-room. It was packed and noisy. He asked about The

Bookstack and her work. Safe ground, Anabelle decided, and talked at length on a subject she loved. He seemed impressed. She believed him when he said he looked forward to Sunday and to meeting Joanna.

When it was time to leave and, she surmised, he judged her sober, they walked to her car. He unlocked it for her before returning her keys. As she drove away, she glanced in her rear-view mirror. He was clearly visible. A still, black figure, illuminated by the bright car park lights. She watched him watching her until she turned the corner.

4

"MARK DALGETTI knows exactly what he's doing," Anabelle thought. "He's nobody's fool." She was packing her suitcase to leave for Ischia and reflecting on the way he had charmed both her and Joanna over Sunday lunch. Joanna was so impressed by his intelligence and good manners that Anabelle began to doubt her own mistrust of his motives. Yet, she had seen the ruthless side of him when he was crossed. Joanna hadn't. In fact, during that lunch, Mark and Joanna seemed to be getting on so well, discussing business and politics, that Anabelle left them to it. She made the coffee and did the washing-up, tactfully giving them a chance to talk about her.

Mark told them something of his own family. He was half-Italian. His father, now dead, came from Naples, though his mother was English and this gave the connection with the Cavendish family. His mother's people and the Cavendish family had been friends. She had since remarried and moved to America. It also transpired that Mark's father and Rupert Cavendish had been partners in several ventures and that Paul's sister Eleanor—Anabelle's aunt —had never married and she lived with her father on Ischia.

The arrangements for Anabelle's trip were made within the next week. Joanna took on extra part-time help at The Bookstack and Anabelle hurriedly shopped for a few additions to her wardrobe. She didn't possess much in the way of "resort" clothes, so she bought some cotton separates and a pretty shirt-dress in soft sugared-almond checks for any formal occasions. Anabelle began to feel almost holidayish!

Sadly, she would be away for Joanna's birthday, but promised to phone on the day. The hiding place of her négligée set could remain a secret until then.

Joanna kindly offered to drive her to Lanstead Marina on the day of her departure, but Anabelle declined, preferring to say her goodbyes at home.

Anabelle paid off her taxi and stood beside her suitcase on the waterfront at

Lanstead. It was six o'clock in the evening and the setting sun sent rays of red through the wispy clouds. A cool breeze was blowing up and she was glad of her Shetland sweater over her shirt and jeans. Mark was there to meet her as arranged. He also wore jeans, and a practical guernsey in traditional navy blue. He looked as handsome as ever.

"Hello." he said cheerily. "I appreciate your punctuality. I want to sail on the evening tide."

He picked up her suitcase and directed her along the stone jetty to a deep water berth.

Lanstead Marina was at the head of an inlet and Anabelle knew they would have to negotiate Lanstead Creek before reaching the open sea. She had formed a mental image of the motor yacht in which she would travel based on the craft she had seen locally. Therefore, she was quite speechless when she saw it. It looked brand new. Trust Mark to own such a magnificent vessel!

It was moored with its stern to the jetty, cheek by jowl with similar, though not such opulent craft. Its sleek white bow pointed arrow-like towards the open sea.

Above the waterline, a row of small round portholes punctuated the smooth hull. The forward deck was clear and uncluttered, accentuating the sharp. cutting bow, while amidships, high deck-housing sported large rectangular, curtained windows. On top of the deck-housing a closed-in wheelhouse carried an impressive array of transmitter aerials on its roof.

Anabelle stared. The name painted boldly on the bow was *Dalgetti III*.

"Is it yours?" she asked surprised. She had assumed, for some reason, the yacht in which she was to travel would belong to her grandfather.

He replied, "Only in as much as I designed her. She belongs to the company."

"Rupert Cavendish's company?"

"Mine, actually," he answered shortly. He took her elbow and led her to the stern, then guided her across the narrow roped gangplank connecting the yacht to the jetty. As he helped her down on to the afterdeck, he smiled and said, "Welcome aboard, Anabelle."

"Thanks." She felt breathless. Her pulse raced and her stomach fluttered at his light touch on her arm. She put it down to nerves as the excitement of the pending sea voyage crept over her. She swallowed and said, "Did you say we were sailing on the *evening* tide?" She thought they would stay in dock the first night, to unpack and settle in.

He nodded. "Otherwise we have to wait a whole twelve hours for the next."

"But at night? In the dark?"

He laughed. "You *are* an inexperienced sailor, aren't you? There's absolutely no need to worry. The *Dalgetti III* is equipped with the very latest in navigational aids and radio. She's had extensive coastal trials and, I assure you, she's quite safe."

Of course, she must be, Anabelle thought. Yet she couldn't help feeling uneasy.

"Now, I'll take you to your cabin. All the guest-cabins and crew accommodation are below. This way."

Anabelle followed him into the dim

interior of the saloon. A thick firm carpet covered the floor. There was a polished mahogany banister in the corner of the saloon. It hid, discreetly, the top stair of a short flight of steps that led below. Anabelle padded after him.

"I've put you in the largest guest-cabin," he went on. "It's a double and has its own private bathroom. I think you'll find everything to your satisfaction. I suggest you unpack now and settle in while we cast off. I shall be fully occupied for a while navigating the harbour and creek." He smiled at her, a spontaneous wide smile which showed his even white teeth. "Perhaps, when you're ready," he concluded, "you'd like to come up to the wheelhouse. The view is worth seeing when we approach the open sea."

The open sea. A shiver of excitement ran through Anabelle. Mark left her and she wandered, fascinated, around the compact, well-designed cabin. There were two portholes in the main cabin and another two in the adjoining bathroom. All were adorned by pretty off-white lace curtains. Idly, she fingered the sleek satin of the bedcover. Its old-gold colour echoed the fitted carpet.

She unpacked and took her toilet things into the bathroom to wash. It was while she was brushing her hair that she sensed the dull throb of the boat's engines.

Suddenly she felt incredibly alone and insecure. This was the point of no return, she realised. She was on her way to meet her grandfather. A flutter of panic clutched her stomach and she suddenly wished she had stayed at home. She thought of Joanna, and the portrait that was rightly hers, and her grandfather's autocracy, and stilled her panic with determination. She would present a bold and noble front to Rupert Cavendish. She would show him what an excellent job Joanna had done in bringing her up alone. Anabelle squared her shoulders. She would start practising now.

When she made her way back on deck, they were already well on their way down Lanstead Creek. The tide was ebbing. The Marina was receding fast. Two swans by the bank bobbed gently in the widening wake of *Dalgetti III*. Anabelle climbed the steep steps to the boat deck and bridge. Through the glass door of the wheelhouse, she saw Mark sitting on a high stool at the wheel. He was surrounded by a confusing array of electronic dials and equipment.

He glanced over his shoulder as she slid open the door. "Ah, Anabelle," he remarked. "So you found your way all right. I'll be with you in just a second."

She slid the door shut behind her. "The *Dalgetti III* is a beautiful boat."

"Mmm. I like her," he murmured absently without looking round. He stretched forward, peering at one of the illuminated green dials, and flicked a switch. The action flexed the muscles of his back and pulled at the fine wool of his guernsey.

Anabelle watched him run his fingers through his unruly black hair and stretch again. "Where are the others?" she asked lightly.

"The others?"

"The rest of the crew?"

He reached to shift a lever. "I'll explain in a minute when we're clear of creek hazards."

She gazed around the wheelhouse. It

was mainly composed of glass on all sides. The technical instrumentation was set in burnished glowing mahogany. Nearby, a chart-table was covered in sea-going maps and littered with perspex navigation aids; set squares, dividers, things that Anabelle hadn't seen since geometry lessons at school.

Mark straightened his broad shoulders and swivelled on the stool to face her. He looked directly into her wide grey eyes with a dispassionate expression. "I've already told you. The delay in *Dalgetti III's* departure caused a few hitches. The skipper's been sent on to Italy to sort them out."

"And the rest of the crew?" Anabelle prompted.

He grinned. "Don't panic. I'm at least as good as the skipper when it comes to handling boats. My personal assistant, Ali, was to have been on board—"

"Was to have?" she interrupted.

"She had to return to Italy, too," he explained patiently. "There's a lot of preparation for the Press launching of *Dalgetti III* when I get her home." He paused and reflected, "I shall miss Ali. She's an excellent cook."

"But where are the others?" Anabelle pressed.

"What others?"

"Don't be evasive, Mark," she snapped. "I mean the other crew members." She knew the answer before he gave it.

"There are no others. The *Dalgetti III* is designed to be handled with the minimum of manpower. One working couple can provide a comfortable lifestyle for—"

"Spare me the sales talk!"

She despaired of him. Why on earth didn't he mention this earlier? There was a stool hinged underneath the knee hole- of the chart-table. She swung it out and sank thankfully on to it. Why had he deliberately deceived her?

"You misled me on purpose," she said flatly.

"No. I didn't." He sounded indignant. "You misunderstood, so don't put the blame on me."

She took a deep breath. "You said you were shorthanded. You gave the impression that I would simply have to help out a bit."

"And that's the truth. I had hoped to be fully crewed, but circumstances overtook me."

"There was a man in here when I boarded," she argued. "What happened to him?"

He shrugged. "He was just a man from the boatyard, checking her over for me."

"But I naturally assumed—"

"You assume too much, Anabelle," he bit back. "First you assume there's a price on your head, that I'm out to capture at all costs, then that I've duped you into coming aboard with me! What do you think I am? Some kind of twentieth century pirate?" He sighed and massaged the back of his neck in a gesture of irritation that further dishevelled his untidy hair. "Let's get one thing straight before we go any further," he added tightly. "Are you quite sure you want to go to Italy?"

"Yes, but—"

"Yes, but? Either you do, or you don't!"

Anabelle gritted her teeth to keep her

93

temper. "You know perfectly well I expected a larger party on board!"

"What you really mean," he retaliated, "is that you don't trust me."

"Since you've mentioned it—no."

"I see. You don't like the idea of being alone with me for the duration of the voyage."

"You've got it in one," she retorted. "But don't flatter yourself it's you personally, Mark. I'd be just as cautious with any man I didn't know very well."

"Flatter?" he flung back sarcastically. It seemed to amuse him in a twisted kind of way. "It proves I'm right about one thing. You *are* worried about your virtue. How quaint!"

"Not quaint," she flashed. "Just sensible!"

"And insulting to my integrity," he returned angrily. "Let's suppose I do have designs on you, shall we? What makes you think I'd force my attentions where they weren't wanted? Don't worry, Anabelle. Beautiful though you are, your virtue's safe with me." He paused significantly and lowered his voice. "If that's what *you* want, of course. It takes two, you know." He raised a questioning eyebrow.

There was a long heavy silence while they eyed each other belligerently. Then Mark swung back to the controls and said, "Well, now we understand each other, we can relax and enjoy the trip."

"Enjoy?" She laughed incredulously. "You seem to forget, this isn't a holiday for me. From what I've heard of my grandfather, it isn't going to be much fun."

"Then why did you come?"

Anabelle chewed her lip thoughtfully. Curiosity? Certainly, but mainly for Joanna's sake really, for the lost years and the doubt. It was difficult to put into words.

"For the valuable portrait?" Mark suggested.

"No!" She was stung by his taunt. "We don't need his gifts! We don't need him!"

Mark pushed down a lever and flicked a switch. Anabelle heard a change in the engine throb as they slowed. He swung round, his face a grim mask. "Then perhaps we'd better turn back now. It was never my intention to bring an object of

95

retribution to Rupert. He's an old man who wants to make amends and reaffirm his affection for his only grandchild."

"While continuing to hate the mother of that child," she added for him.

"He has good reason to."

"Because she took me away?" Anabelle threw out her hands to emphasise her point. "My mother took me away from him for my sake, because she loved me. Not to purposefully inflict pain on Rupert."

She saw a muscle clench in Mark's shadowy jaw. "No," he replied curtly. "She'd already caused enough pain taking his only son from him by her—her—" He stopped short, as though he'd said too much.

"By her what?" Anabelle demanded, rising to her feet. "By her love for him? Does Rupert still blame my mother for the fact that my father left home?"

Mark kept his eyes on the sun-reddened sky through the windshield. The creek had widened as the land slid away and the open sea beckoned.

"Calm down, Anabelle." Mark exhaled

slowly and his shoulders sagged. "Let's leave the past where it belongs: forgotten."

Certainly. Anabelle had no desire to dig up old grudges, but neither could she stand by and let her mother be misjudged so. Then suddenly, in front of them, a flock of geese flew across the sky. They flapped silently in formation, distant dark shapes against the darkening clouds. Their attention was diverted, the strain eased.

"Would you like a drink?" Mark suggested. "I certainly would. It's been quite a day. I expect you would too."

It sounded a good idea. She agreed. She hadn't meant for them to get off to a bad start like this. She sighed.

"We'll be clear of the creek soon," he informed her. "I'll anchor in the shallows and fix us an aperitif." They were moving faster again. He glanced over his shoulder and raised one straight black eyebrow. "Unless you'd care to take the controls while I go below now?"

"No, thanks!" She managed a grin. "Tell me where the drinks are and I'll get them."

"I was hoping you'd volunteer. They're in the main saloon, in the long sideboard. I'll have a large gin and tonic. Very large."

Anabelle welcomed the diversion and slipped out quickly. They were in the estuary now and land seemed a long way away in the gathering gloom of the evening. She paused on the sundeck and watched the wash from the fast cutting bow fan out from either side of the boat. She wondered how far he planned to sail before anchoring for the night. How long would it take them to reach Ischia; how long would she be cooped up with this attractive, yet disturbing man?

She gripped the handrail tightly as she went down the steps to the main deck. Her stomach churned uncomfortably. She wasn't used to the constant rolling motion of the sea. The evening air was chilly and she shivered.

By contrast, the saloon with its thick carpet was warm.

There was a good selection of drinks and Anabelle poured out two gin and tonics— a large one and a small one.

"Thanks," Mark said sincerely as she rejoined him.

Anabelle sat at the chart-table.

"Come over here. I can't talk to you properly over there." He pulled out a foldaway seat adjacent to his.

She hesitated for a second, then slid on to the stool beside him.

"The tide pulls westwards in this part of the Channel," he explained. "And it works to our advantage. I'm keeping close to land so that we can find a sheltered spot to anchor for the night. Are you hungry yet? I'd like to make decent headway before we stop to eat."

"No. I'm not hungry at all." In fact, the mention of food was particularly unwelcome. The sea made her feel queasy. "How long will it take us to reach Ischia?" she asked, to keep her mind on something else.

"That depends," he murmured.

"On what?"

"Lots of things."

Damn him! He was being evasive again. She wasn't interested in verbal ping-pong. She stood up and moved away saying, "I asked a simple question. Can't you give a straight answer?"

"Come back here, Anabelle," he ordered.

She ignored him.

"Now." An ominous, threatening tone had entered his voice. "Do as I say, Anabelle," he added.

"Why?" she retaliated.

"Because we're at sea and you're inexperienced and that could mean danger." He sounded angry with her. "Listen to me, you stubborn little fool. That sea out there is very real! If I ask you to do something, you do it! You do it immediately and ask questions later. Do I make myself clear?"

He turned to face her. His green eyes pierced challengingly into hers. Of course, she could see the sense in what he said. But it didn't apply now. There were no pressing dangers at the moment. He was simply using the situation as an excuse to show his masculine superiority. Well, she thought, if it pleased his inflated ego, she'd comply. Anything for a quiet life.

"Aye aye, Captain." She saluted

smartly, smiled sweetly, and dutifully slid on to the stool beside him.

"Skipper, if you don't mind."

Mind? She didn't give a damn what she called him. Preferably nothing at all, she thought. It was becoming increasingly obvious that to survive this voyage, she was going to have to stay well clear of Mark Dalgetti. Still, she hadn't expected a holiday, had she?

He let her exaggerated sigh pass without comment and went on patiently, "While you were getting the drinks, there was a shipping forecast on the radio. It sounds as if we'll be in for some rough weather when we leave the Channel tomorrow. If that's the case, I don't want you out on deck alone. You stay below unless you're with me. Do you understand?"

She nodded. "Yes, OK." It suited her fine.

"Good. In view of the weather, I'd like to make as much headway as possible while the sea's calm. If necessary, we'll cruise through the night."

"What?" Anabelle's eyes widened in horror. That sounded crazy to her.

"Don't panic," he soothed, "you'll sleep

like a baby after all this sea air." He spun the wheel and Anabelle's stomach lurched as they changed direction.

"There's a shallow stretch coming up. It'll provide a suitable anchorage while we eat."

They were moving quite fast down the coast and seemed, to Anabelle, to be a long way from shore. Lights winked on the land as darkness fell. An eerie beam flashed regularly on the horizon from a distant revolving lighthouse.

But it was the silence of the sea that impressed Anabelle most of all. When Mark stilled the engines and dropped anchor, the only sound was the soft swish of water on the hull as they gently rode the waves and the night closed in.

They climbed down a ladder to the galley. It was larger than she'd imagined and gleamed like the interior of a space ship. All white and stainless steel with black glass in some of the appliances; it was sparkling new. As well as a conventional fridge and cooker, there was a small deep-freeze and microwave oven. Everything had been thought of for convenience and comfort in cooking.

Mark pulled off his guernsey and rolled back the cuffs of a blue denim shirt to reveal sinewy, tanned forearms. He seemed equally at home in the galley as he had been in the wheelhouse. He took some boxes of salad vegetables from the fridge and dumped them on the stainless steel sink.

"Shall I do that?" she volunteered.

"Sure," he agreed readily. "What shall we eat with it?"

Together they peered into the deep-freeze to choose something they both liked. As they stood side by side, Anabelle became increasingly aware of the warmth of his body next to hers. Her eyes were drawn to his strong smooth throat visible through the open neck of his shirt. He reached across her to move a package and their bodies touched, sending a charge of electricity coursing through Anabelle.

She moved away instinctively. He stopped what he was doing and turned to look at her. There was a puzzled expression in his shrewd green eyes. Despite the cold air from the freezer on her face, Anabelle felt a blush rise to her cheeks.

She blushed because he'd noticed. Their contact had lasted for a few seconds only, yet her reaction had been immediate: a reflex action, away from him, away from danger, and he'd detected it. He watched her steadily as her face flamed, then continued to remove the pack of frozen food.

"Chicken Maryland," he said lightly. "OK with you?"

The moment was over, she breathed again. "Fine." She nodded.

Their meal was quickly prepared in the microwave. They carried the plates of food through to the mahogany table in the adjacent saloon. It tasted good, but Anabelle couldn't eat much. Nor could she finish the Californian wine that Mark opened. She tried, then pushed her plate away with an apology.

"I'm afraid I feel a bit queasy," she admitted.

He frowned. "It might take you a few days to find your sea-legs. Do you usually suffer from seasickness?"

"I've never been to sea before, so I can't say." She managed a weak grin.

"Would some coffee help?"

"I don't know."

He stood up. "I'll put some on."

"No. Finish your dinner first. I'll do it." She took her uneaten meal out to the galley and scraped it away.

She filled the coffee-maker with water and switched it on, then spooned the grounds into the paper cone. Mark followed her shortly afterwards. He glanced keenly in her direction and started the washing-up. Anabelle took a cloth and listlessly began to dry. She knew he was watching her, and frowning.

The coffee was ready when they'd finished. Mark poured a cup and handed it to her with narrowed eyes.

"You look a bit pasty," he commented. "How do you feel?"

"Weak." She shrugged. "Tired, I suppose. It's been a long day and I'm not used to the sea." She put her coffee mug down on the sink. "I'm sorry, I can't drink this."

"You'd better have an early night," he

advised. "I'm going to weigh anchor straightaway and cruise on further. Have you got everything you need?"

"Yes, thanks."

"Good. Well, I hope you'll feel better in the morning."

She staggered below. When she looked in the mirror, she thought that "a bit pasty" was an understatement. Ashen, more like. Her hair had lost its bounce and sheen in the sea air, and she'd pushed the resulting frizz behind her ears. She began to hate her reflection.

A bed had never been more welcome. She fell into it and closed her eyes in an attempt to shut out the dull throb of the engines. Even when they were anchored, there was an intermittent buzz from the generators in the engine-room. She assumed she'd get used to it in time.

But would she get used to Mark Dalgetti?

There was an aura about him that she found disturbing, in a sensational kind of way. Without doubt, he was a sexually attractive man. Tall and broad-shouldered, though sinewy rather than overtly muscular, he moved with the wound-up energy of an athlete.

He was not conventionally handsome. Anabelle thought his face too lean and hard for that, yet he possessed a sensual magnetism which she couldn't ignore—in spite of his irritating, overbearing manner. But, he could be so arrogant at times, she fumed suddenly, and so charming when it suited him! He knew he was attractive to women.

A ruthless man, she concluded, who uses any means available to get what he wants. Sweet reason or brute force, it was all the same to him just as long as things went his way.

Well, his methods needn't include her! He might be skipper on board *Dalgetti III*, and she'd have to be subservient to his authority while they were afloat. But, as soon as they reached Ischia, his job would be over and she could say goodbye to him. Anabelle had her own ideas about this visit to her grandfather, and she wouldn't be swayed by anything Mark Dalgetti had to contribute!

So, until they got to Ischia, she would stay well out of his way, she decided. It wouldn't be difficult, especially if she didn't feel well! She had a tailor-made excuse for staying in her cabin. In fact, hadn't he warned her to do just that if the weather turned rough?

Although Anabelle didn't exactly pray for bad weather, she could see there would be advantages if Mark was fully occupied sailing the boat. It would be easy to stay out of his way and avoid any further hassle.

5

SHE shouldn't have tempted Providence. When she awoke next morning she gazed out of her porthole at a grey, swelling sea.

Her head was muzzy and her legs weak, but she showered and dressed. The queasiness increased. Mind over matter! she told herself sternly, pulling on a clean shirt and jeans. It was simply a question of getting used to the motion of the boat. What she needed was a little bracing fresh air to clear her head! She shrugged into her jersey and made her way to the boatdeck.

The sky was as grey as the sea and its unfriendliness depressed her. The wind buffeted around her ears, catching her long golden hair and whipping a touch of colour into her pale cheeks. Through the glass door of the wheelhouse, she saw Mark. He was standing at the wheel, watching the turbulent horizon. His head turned sharply as she slid open the door.

"'Morning, Anabelle," he called, raising

his voice against the whistling wind. "Feel any better?"

"Yes, thanks," she lied, closing off the noisy weather smartly. Spray spattered on to the glass windshield over the controls. She wandered over to stand beside him.

He glanced quickly in her direction. "You look a bit livelier this morning, anyway," he remarked.

Did she? She didn't feel it. She felt as rough as he looked. And he certainly looked the worse for wear at the moment! There were dark shadows under his eyes as though he hadn't slept a wink. And he needed a shave. A blue-black haze coarsened his jaw.

"Have you been here all night?" she queried. She stifled an impulse to lean across and straighten his collar. It was half-in, half-out of his Guernsey as if he'd dressed in a hurry.

"I managed to snatch three or four hours sleep." He rasped his hand over his stubbly chin. "I didn't think you'd be up at this hour. It's very early."

A large swell slammed against the hull and Mark heaved on the wheel to hold their course.

"What's the forecast?" Anabelle asked, tentatively holding on to the control console for support.

He noticed and grinned crookedly. "You'll be all right. *Dalgetti III*'s an ocean-going vessel. She's got the best stabilisers money can buy."

"Is it going to get any worse?"

"Can't say. If it does, we'll put into port. But, until then, I want to cover as much distance as possible. She's got a deadline to meet in the Mediterranean."

"I see." Anabelle grimaced at the waves through the salt-spattered glass. The sky was darkening ominously with each passing minute. "Have you had breakfast yet?" She guessed he hadn't.

"No. I've been tied up here. I ought to stay on the bridge in weather like this."

"Shall I bring you something up?" she offered.

"Thanks. That sounds like a good idea."

"Anything in particular?"

He didn't need to think. He replied immediately, "A big mug of coffee and a toasted ham sandwich. There's an infrared toaster in the galley and—"

"Yes, I noticed yesterday. Don't worry, I'll find my way around."

In the galley, she located the bread, took the cold cooked ham out of the fridge and put on the coffee. The smell of the grounds wafted up at her. Normally, she relished them, but now she found them repugnant. The boat rolled slightly. She placed a hand on the shiny steel sink as a wave of nausea swept over her. Several minutes passed before she was able to continue.

It wasn't until she began slicing the ham that Anabelle admitted to herself that the feeling wasn't going to subside. She felt awful and her head was peculiarly giddy. She held her body rigid as the boat rolled again.

She sat down on the galley stool and took several deep breaths to control herself. The nausea went away—marginally. She tackled the ham again and the giddiness returned. This time she closed her eyes and prayed. Her arms and legs felt like lead. She opened her eyes again and the ham sat there, challenging her.

She dragged the stool to the work-surface and picked up the knife. It was a heavy carving knife and her grip was weak. It clattered noisily from her hand.

"Take care! That's sharp." Mark's strong deep voice made her jump. "I just came down to say . . ." He stopped, obviously realising something was wrong. "Anabelle, are you all right?"

She pulled herself together and tried to pick up the fallen knife. The next moment he was beside her, prising it from her fingers and turning her face to the light.

"Oh, poor Anabelle," he groaned slowly. "You're green."

"It's nothing," she protested. "I expect it'll go off in a bit." She wanted to laugh and cry at the same time, and the result was a mildly hysterical giggle.

He took her face in his hands and rebuked her mildly. "You must have felt ill earlier. Why on earth didn't you say, you silly little idiot?"

She shook her head weakly. "I didn't think it would last."

Mark muttered something she guessed was derogatory and rummaged in the first-aid box where he found some foil-wrapped pills. "Take a couple of those," he ordered.

He poured out a glass of mineral water and Anabelle swallowed the pills.

"They're the best treatment I know for seasickness," he explained. "But they're strong. They'll stop you from being sick, but they'll make you very drowsy in the process."

"Thanks," she croaked. "I'm afraid I do feel rather bad."

He frowned. "You look awful. I'd better get you to bed before you feel any worse."

"Yes, you're right," she agreed. She struggled to her feet and her knees buckled beneath her.

Mark shot across the galley and caught her just in time to prevent her falling. She swayed dizzily, clawing at a handful of his sweater, and felt his body brace to support her. He was like a rock, she thought. A warm, welcome rock.

"Steady, Anabelle. OK, I've got you." He sounded sympathetic. "Come on, I'll help you down to your cabin."

"I'm all right," she insisted, though weakly. "I can manage."

"The hell you can," he growled. "You

really are quite stupidly stubborn some-times!"

"But you can't leave the wheel! I mean —shouldn't you be up there, on the bridge?" She had visions of them out of control, drifting helplessly at sea.

"Why not let me worry about that?" he replied firmly. He placed a strong supportive arm around her shoulders, and added, "Haven't you heard of automatic pilot?"

Yes, Anabelle had. But, if the truth were known, she was past caring. She craved the oblivion of sleep to release her from this dreadful persistent nausea.

He half-carried her to her cabin and, when they were inside, steered her resolutely towards the bed. She groaned and sat down. She closed her eyes but the furni-ture still floated, inside her head.

Mark's far-away voice ordered, "Get into bed, Anabelle."

"In a minute," she murmured. "Just give me a minute."

"No. Now." He sounded firm. "After those pills you'll be out cold in a short time. If you fall asleep like that you'll feel even worse when you wake up. Get into bed now!"

"All right, all right, don't bully me," she muttered. She appreciated the sense in what he said, but she hadn't lost all her judgment. She felt ghastly, yes, but she wasn't completely witless. However ill she was, she wanted him out of her cabin before she undressed for bed. With a great effort she lifted her head and opened her eyes.

"Just as soon as you've left," she added quietly and clearly.

He was staring at her, very intently. "OK," he agreed. "Let me see you capable of standing on your own two feet and then I'll leave." He moved to the door and placed his hand on the knob. But he kept his eyes on her.

The cabin lights seemed too bright for Anabelle. She screwed up her face to protect her eyes. Why wouldn't he go? she wondered. She reached across the bed, removed her nightdress from underneath the pillow and staggered to her feet.

"Satisfied?" she queried hoarsely.

It was too ambitious a movement. The walls spun, her head reeled and she lost her balance. She broke her fall, luckily, on the bed, hitting the cold silky cover with a bump.

Mark was beside her almost immediately, rolling her over, supporting her in a sitting position. She lolled against him as the last vestiges of her energy drained away.

"See where your stubbornness gets you?" he goaded, not unsympathetically. "The sooner you're in bed, the better." He took hold of the bottom of her jersey and, in one smooth, deft action, lifted it over her head.

Her flaccid arms could offer no resistance, although she tried to make a weak attempt to push him away.

"I can manage," she protested.

"No, you can't," he said, as if it were a well-known statement of fact. He started to undo the buttons of her shirt. His hands moved quickly in their task. They were surprisingly gentle. The shirt slid easily from her back. He eased her forward to start undoing the hook of her bra. Her cheek lay against his chest and the wool of his sweater was rough on her skin. He handled her clinically, as a doctor would a sick child, yet still she shivered at his touch. For, sick or not, his face told her that he was not indifferent to her body— nor was she to his hands on her.

"Please don't," she croaked. "I—I can do it. But I can't undress while you're here."

"I appreciate your modesty," he responded quietly. "It's a refreshing change these days."

His voice was low, but tinged with roughness. As he talked, he picked up her nightdress and dropped it over her head so that she could remain decent while she removed her bra.

"Please go now," she muttered. "I can do the rest."

In answer he sank to his knees and began undoing the laces on her canvas training-shoes. He took them off, then removed her socks and turned his back to place them neatly under a chair. This gave her a chance to slip out of her jeans and into bed, for, clearly, he would not leave until she had done so. He folded her clothes in a tidy pile before he looked at her again.

And, though he smiled, the tension was still there in his eyes.

Anabelle managed a weak smile in return. "Thank you," she said, "I feel better already." She settled into the soft comforting pillow and closed her eyes. What a silly, helpless picture she must present, she thought remorsefully; clad in a pink gingham nightie with a high neck and frilly hem, she was not the kind of girl he was used to undressing, she was sure.

In a moment of speculation she imagined the type of woman who belonged in a cabin like this. She saw a tall, tanned model with raven-black hair, dressed in silk. The comparison with herself was laughable and, in her weakened state, a feeble hysterical giggle escaped from her throat.

"Humour in adversity?" Mark commented with raised eyebrows, as he tucked the sheets in round her. "That's a rare quality."

"If I didn't laugh, I'd cry," she muttered sourly in response.

He smoothed her hair back from her temples in a cooling, soothing manner and said, "Try to sleep. The tablets will help you."

She glanced at him, turning her head, and her cheek brushed his palm. She saw the fire again leap into his eyes and she wondered what might have happened in different circumstances, if she had not been ill. For, despite his matter-of-fact approach in putting her to bed, she had detected the suppressed tension in him when he touched her. And all the time she had been acutely aware of his powerful masculinity.

"I must get back to the bridge," he continued evenly. "If the weather gets any worse, I'll put into port, I promise you." He slipped quietly from the cabin, leaving her alone.

Her eyelids drooped. The drugs were taking effect. She drifted away with thoughts of Mark on her mind. He'd said she was beautiful, hadn't he? He'd found her attractive, hadn't he?

When she woke up, her watch had stopped and she'd lost track of the time. The engines droned and the rain spattered against the darkened portholes. It wasn't night, though. The black clouds rolled ominously outside the glass and the sight of them brought on the familiar nauseating giddiness. She turned away and switched on the bedhead light.

On her bedside table was a carton of foil-wrapped seasick pills and a bottle of mineral water and a glass. Mark must have brought them in when she was asleep. She took two more tablets and tried to read. But her eyelids felt like lead, and she slept on and off, oblivious to time, for the rest of the day.

The next thing she knew, someone was urgently calling her name. Mark was standing at the foot of the bed, holding a tray. It was very dark outside the portholes and Anabelle's immediate reaction was that she felt better. She levered herself into a sitting position.

"I've heated some soup for you," Mark said, placing the tray by her bed. "You ought to eat something, even if you don't feel like it. It'll help keep up your strength."

"Thanks. I'll try. I might even get up."

"I wouldn't advise it. The roll of the boat is less down here and it's best to keep your head below the porthole so you can't see the swell of the waves. It could be psychological, you know. Just the sight of a moving sea makes some people feel ill."

Anabelle shrugged ruefully. "I thought maybe a breath of fresh air—"

"No. I'd rather you didn't go up on deck, particularly as you're in a weakened state. I've got my hands full handling the boat in this weather. You'd only be an added worry."

"All right," she agreed.

There was no reason for him to stay in her cabin any longer. Yet he stood by her bed for what seemed a long time, staring at her. His expression was impassive. Anabelle returned his gaze for a few seconds but, unable to hold it, made a pretence of straightening the sheets and the sleeves of her nightdress.

Finally, he seemed to realise her mild embarrassment and asked solicitously, "Is there anything else you want?"

She raised her wide grey eyes candidly to his and replied, "How about some *terra firma?*" She was serious. That's what she'd been thinking about most of all during her waking moments. But she saw the humour of the situation and grinned.

He grinned back, releasing the uneasiness between them. "Yes, I know. The wind is against us and we're not making much headway. I'm steering for a sheltered bay for the night. If the gales haven't dropped by tomorrow, we'll go ashore."

"Thanks." She smiled.

"I'm glad you're feeling better."

"How do you know I am?" She certainly hadn't said as much.

"You look it. Don't let the soup go cold."

When he'd gone, she scrambled out of bed to go to the bathroom. She peered in the mirror. She did look better. There was a sparkle back in her grey eyes and her skin was clearer.

The soup was pleasant; a mild broth of indeterminate flavour with some plain, dry rusks. She ate them gingerly, felt the boat pitch and climbed nervously into bed. She yawned widely. How could she sleep so much? It must be the pills, she thought drowsily and snuggled under the sheets.

Then it was light, and morning, and she knew the worst was over. The sky was washed out and pale, but the sea relatively calm and it had stopped raining. Anabelle turned on the shower and looked out some fresh clothes.

She was standing under the hot water, rinsing her hair, when she became aware of a heavy thudding on her cabin door. Mark was calling her name loudly. What on earth was the panic? she wondered. A frisson of fear ran through her. An emergency? Were they sinking? A fire? Hurriedly, she stepped out of the shower and wrapped a large bath-sheet, sarong-style, round her body. She had neither dressing-gown nor slippers. They were still next door by the bed.

The rapping was now on her bathroom door and Mark was calling her name more urgently. She wrenched open the door and almost collided with him, crying, "What's wrong?"

He froze. The carton of pills that she'd left on the bedside table was in his right hand. For a second he just looked at her, seemingly lost for words, and inhaling deeply.

Then he said, "I knocked several times on your cabin door and didn't get an answer." He gestured with the carton. "I wasn't sure how many of these you'd taken. Too many can be dangerous."

Anabelle clutched at the towel around her, too aware of her naked shoulders and the way Mark's eyes were travelling along them. Her heart missed a beat and a warning bell rang in her head.

"I appreciate your concern," she said, injecting a frosty note to her voice. "But really I'm fine now. Honestly. The nausea's gone completely."

"Then why on earth didn't you answer me?" he raged suddenly.

She blinked, surprised at his anger. "I'm sorry. I didn't hear you until you shouted. I was under the shower. Didn't you hear the water running?"

"Of course I did," he snapped. "You might have answered me even so. You could have been unconscious on the floor, for all I knew!"

"Well, I'm not. I'm fine."

His green eyes glowed vibrantly. In the morning light he looked very much alive; clean-shaven, fresh, his skin glowing healthily against the blue denim of an open-necked shirt.

His glance flickered over her; from her scrubbed face and hair to the droplets of water clinging to her satin smooth skin. A warning bell rang again and she sidled past him.

"Those pills are strong," he went on tightly. "I had some difficulty in waking you yesterday and I thought you might have taken some more."

"I did," she admitted. "But I only took two. Really, Mark! I am old enough to take care of myself now."

"Are you?" he queried cryptically.

She swallowed. She wanted to get dressed. He could see she was all right so there was no need for him to stay. Yet, he showed no signs of leaving her cabin.

"Yes!" she replied fiercely, "and I think you're taking your job as 'minder' just a little too seriously at the moment!"

His eyes narrowed and he took a threatening step towards her. "What did you call me?"

"Isn't that what you are? A paid heavy to bring me in, by fair means or foul?"

"Is that what you think I am?" As he spoke, he took her arm and roughly pulled her close to his body. His fingers bit into her flesh.

She looked up at him and saw desire in his eyes. Despite the pain, her heart fluttered and her pulse jumped unsteadily.

"Please, Mark," she begged, "I'd like to get dressed."

"Would you?" His voice was very low and he shook his head slightly. "Somehow, I don't think so."

A hand fell on her other arm and she felt imprisoned by him, but she didn't struggle. What's more, she realised she didn't want to! And one glance at his face told her that he knew. *He knew.*

"I—I warned you, Mark," she protested weakly, clutching at straws. "I warned you at the hotel. If you put a foot wrong, you'll have to answer to my grandfather and I'm sure—"

"Do you really think a threat like that would temper my actions?" He smiled triumphantly. "You underestimate me, Anabelle."

No, she realised in a split second. She didn't. He was ruthless, capable of anything.

"I'll show you what I think of your idle

127

warnings, Miss Anabelle Cavendish!" he mocked.

"I am *not* a Cav—"

She was silenced. His mouth closed over hers and, although he had dragged her roughly to him, his lips were gentle. She inhaled the clean smooth texture of his skin, smelt of soap. She revelled in the resilience of his body, the breadth of him, the firmness, the strength. He intoxicated her. The sheer sensuality of his arms around her stimulated reactions in her which she found alarmingly powerful. She stretched on tiptoe as he held her closer, his hands pressing on her back and his kisses becoming more hard and demanding. She knew she must stop him, if only she could find the will.

Against all her better judgment, she wound her arms around his body and she yielded. For those few snatched seconds it seemed they were as one person. Then, suddenly, they were apart.

He let her go. No, more than that, she realised, he pushed her away—roughly. He was breathing rapidly and deeply, and his voice was hoarse.

"Tell that to your grandfather, if you dare!" he growled.

Anabelle was shaken; shaken to the core by the strength of her own response to Mark's advances.

"I shall!" she cried in answer. "My warning wasn't idle! I meant it! Every word."

But she was lying now, as she had before. Of course she wouldn't go running to her grandfather.

"Go on, then!" Mark yelled at her. "Tell him!" His green eyes flashed in his flushed, heated face as he continued, "and maybe I'll tell him a few home truths about how unresisting his darling little granddaughter is!"

"It's a lie!" she denied. "You—you—" she searched for the word to describe his behaviour, and only one sprang to mind, only one fitted—"you *forced* yourself on me!"

"Forced?" He laughed; a harsh, derisory, humourless laugh. "Don't give me that! You wanted me, and you certainly weren't telling me to stop!"

He knew. He was too experienced not to. Why had she acted so foolishly? It was not like her at all. It had happened too quickly for her, and Mark knew what he was doing with women. He needed no lessons, she thought remorsefully.

"It's not the truth," she said. "You were too fast. You didn't even give me a chance to resist."

"Then shall I?"

"Shall you what?"

"Give you another chance to resist?" He raised his straight black eyebrows enquiringly. "Shall I kiss you again and see exactly how far I can get before you beat me off?"

"Now who's making idle threats?" she flung out irritably.

As soon as her words were out, she realised the folly of her challenge. He advanced towards her slowly and she backed nervously away. Her knees connected with the cold silk coverlet of the bed and her legs buckled. She sat down suddenly.

"You—you wouldn't dare," she faltered.

"Wouldn't I?" The situation seemed to amuse him.

She tried not to panic. All she had to do

was keep cool and firmly refuse his approach. He wouldn't get anywhere, she thought fiercely. This time she was ready for him.

He stopped in front of her, so close that her knees touched the denim of his jeans. She tilted her head so that she could look directly into his eyes and said coldly, "Don't touch me, Mark."

His expression didn't alter. His eyelids didn't even flicker. He held her gaze and replied, "I didn't hear you." His lips hardly moved as he spoke. Still holding her gaze, he drew nearer and Anabelle found herself transfixed, unable to move. His lips brushed her soft mouth and, once again, she found she was powerless in his arms.

"Anabelle, you're so beautiful," he breathed.

Once again, she responded to his kisses, her arms went round his neck and she felt weak with longing. While her brain was saying stop, her fingers were twining through his thick black hair.

He shifted slightly, immobilising her with his weight. Then he lifted his head a fraction and whispered treacherously, "I'm right, Anabelle, aren't I? You want me, don't you?"

It was all she needed to restore her sanity. Such arrogance! What a charade all this was! Her fingers tightened in his hair and she yanked his head back.

"All right, Mark," she said abruptly. "You've proved your point. Now, if you've finished playing your nasty little games, I'd like to get dressed."

His face contorted in anger. "You little witch," he seethed, jerking his head free. "I'm certainly not the one who's playing games!"

He moved away from her, and left her feeling cold and bereft. She yearned for his warmth and ached with desire. The cabin echoed with the slam of the door as he departed and gradually the uneven thud of her heart steadied. The tears ran off her cheeks, making dark damp patches on the crumpled silk bedcover. She pulled the towel more closely round her. Why had she been so weak when he first kissed her? Why had she fallen so readily for his obviously well-rehearsed line with women? From the beginning he'd found her attractive, or so he'd said on that very first visit to her flat. Then, at the hotel, he'd told her she was beautiful. And again, just now. Beautiful? No, it wasn't true. She slid off the bed and stood in front of the full-length mirror.

Beautiful girls had tans all the year round. Anabelle's skin was pale and she was too rounded. She gazed critically at her reflection. The tendency to curves was inherited. Joanna was the same. You had to be skinny to be beautiful these days!

She wasn't beautiful. The only thing she could remotely call beautiful was her hair, which was quite a nice golden colour, but otherwise Mark's compliments were all calculated flattery. And for what? she wondered. To curry favour with her so that she'd speak well of him to Rupert? No. His recent behaviour dispelled that idea as soon as it was formed. Then why? For someone to pander to his sexual needs while they were at sea? What had he said about his personal assistant? "I'll miss her, she's a good cook". Were there other services provided by Ali? she asked herself. Immediately, she rebuked her own nosiness. It was none of her business what the relationship was between Mark and Ali, and she didn't really care anyway!

Damn Mark Dalgetti! After the way he'd treated her, he could go and jump in the sea for all she was concerned! She knew exactly how she was going to treat him from now on. Cool. Very cool.

6

SHE was as good as her word. But it was easy, for it appeared that Mark had reached the same decision about the way he would treat her. It was as though they were competing against each other for the gold medal in icy politeness, and it was a relief that he seemed to be avoiding her.

He spent most of his time on the bridge or in the engine-room below decks. He was a man who didn't need much sleep and frequently had breakfasted by the time she got up. They sailed early morning to late evening, exchanging only a few words all day if their paths happened to cross.

However, they always ate together at night after Mark had dropped the anchor in a sheltered bay off shore. He made a point of it but, she guessed, for him it was more a duty than a genuine desire for her company. They made polite conversation, then he excused himself to "finish off some paperwork" in his suite.

Anabelle was aware of frantic arrangements going on. There had been two urgent phone calls on the radio telephone. Once, when she had taken coffee to the wheelhouse, Mark had been engrossed in a staccato exchange in French, and she had beat a hasty retreat.

They missed the worst of the bad weather and, although the sky was overcast and there was a good swell on the dull silver sea, the gales backed and veered north. However, the Bay of Biscay lived up to its reputation for storms, and Anabelle was pleased to discover that she could cope with the roughness and even enjoy the thrill of being afloat.

Then, one morning, Anabelle realised she was too hot in her jeans. She fished out a pair of yellow cotton shorts and a sun-top, and made her way to the boat-deck to sunbathe. The sun loungers were already out between the wheelhouse and the runabout motor launch secured at the stern. Blue sea and sky stretched in every direction; the sun was high and the fresh breeze was warm and caressing on her skin.

Anabelle spread out a towel on one of

the loungers and rummaged in her bag for sun-oil and her current paperback. She could see Mark through the glass door of the wheelhouse. He was standing at the top controls, but he hadn't noticed her. She laid her book on the deck, tipped a little oil into her palms and massaged it over her legs.

She heard the wheelhouse door slide open. Deliberately, she concentrated on her task and didn't look up. Mark bent to pick up the bottle of oil just as she reached for it again. In amazement, her eyes followed the bottle upwards. She had to shade her face from the light. The sun was behind him, and he appeared even darker and wilder than usual.

She couldn't stop her heart missing a beat. His sensuality vibrated towards her. He also wore shorts, but his were frayed and faded denim, and his shirt, which was open to the waist, revealed the glow of his tan. He stood close by her. His long dark legs, lightly veiled in straight black hair, made her own skin seem more deathly white in comparison.

"May I have it back, please?" she asked patiently.

"It's no good," he replied curtly.

Anabelle was indignant. It had been very expensive and was guaranteed to produce a tan. She held out her hand and said, "Well, it certainly isn't any good while it's still in the bottle."

He ran appraising eye over her and idly tossed the bottle of oil from one hand to the other. "You don't want this," he stated. "The sea breeze is deceptive and the sun's rays are strong. You'll fry in this stuff. You need a proper sun-screen to stop you burning."

"Oh, I always go red before I go brown," she informed him.

"You don't have to, if you're prepared to take your time. I'll fetch you some of Ali's sun-screen. You've got a much fairer skin than she has, but it'll be better than nothing."

He went below and returned with a bottle of French lotion. "She swears by this," he explained. "Even so, don't stay in the sun too long. There's plenty of shade on the afterdeck."

"Won't Ali mind my using it?" Anabelle queried.

Mark gave her a mocking smile. "I'll make it up to her, don't worry."

Anabelle blushed at his suggestive tone and he laughed.

"You're burning already." He grinned. "Turn over and I'll put some on your back."

"That won't be necessary. I'm only toasting the front today," she returned coldly. It wasn't true. She wanted to get her legs just a little bit brown all over if she could. But she didn't want him to touch her. Not any more.

"What about your shoulders?" he pointed out. "They're at the right angle to catch the sun."

"I can reach them, thank you."

"Suit yourself." He shrugged and went back to the wheel.

She smoothed the lotion on her throat and shoulders. When she turned over a few minutes later, she tried unsuccessfully to reach her shoulder blades which were exposed by her brief suntop. She'd tied her hair up out of the way, but after several contortions she gave in. She'd have to go inside in a minute anyway as her legs were already beginning to feel prickly from the heat.

The next thing she knew was the startling sensation of cold lotion being dribbled on her back. She cried out in surprise. Mark's hands were firm on her shoulders as they pushed her down.

"Obstinate little mule, aren't you?" he murmured. His fingers manipulated her back and neck; soothing, massaging, relaxing.

Anabelle buried her face in the towel, biting her lip and unable to control the shiver of excitement which ran through her when he was near. She steeled herself to resist him, holding herself rigid.

"Why are you so keyed-up?" he said softly.

How could she say "It's you. The very thought of you winds me up like a spring"? Instead she said, "I guess I'm apprehensive about the future—about Ischia and my grandfather." And it was true.

"You have a few days before then, and they should be exciting ones, to take your mind off your problems. We'll be in Marseilles soon. Ali and Johannes join us there. Johannes is my skipper. He's Dutch."

Anabelle exhaled slowly into the hot damp towel beneath her cheek. She couldn't wait for them to take other people on board.

"That sounds fun," she mumbled, without looking up. Any change was welcome to ease the dreadful impasse that had arisen between them.

"Shall I do your legs?" he queried, trailing a sensuous finger down her arm.

"No, I've had enough," she responded quickly. "I—I mean, I'm too hot, I'd better go inside." Her nerves wouldn't stand any more.

"Perhaps you're right," she heard him say.

She didn't hear the rest. She gathered up her things and fled to her cabin. Her heart was thumping madly as she closed the door. How could she react so feverishly to someone she despised? And what had happened to her resolve to stay cool?

Mark didn't comment on her odd behaviour. He seemed to accept it. Though, later that day, as they prepared dinner together in the galley, she noticed his keen green eyes watching her, analysing her. They heated up *boeuf Bourguignonne* from the freezer and sat at the polished mahogany table in the saloon, mopping up the sauce French fashion with hunks of bread.

She asked lightly, "How much longer shall we be at sea?"

"There's been a slight change of plan," he informed her. "I've decided to put into La Grande Motte near Montpellier. Ali and Johannes will meet us there instead. I know a few people from the resort and we can have a bit of a party on board. Does that appeal to you, Anabelle?"

"Yes," she answered sincerely. "Yes, it does." The atmosphere with just the two of them on *Dalgetti III* had become too claustrophobic for her comfort. He must have realised, she thought. How perceptive of him.

He sat back with his glass of Beaujolais and looked directly at her. "Good." He smiled. "We're sailing into the most inviting summer playground in the world. I'd like you to enjoy it. After Montpellier, the *Dalgetti III* is due in Monte Carlo for Press coverage."

La Grand Motte was a spectacular modern resort offering everything for every sort of water sport. Its huge tiered pyramids of apartment blocks and villas rose in elegant banks above the Marina where a myriad of boats bobbed at their moorings. They anchored off shore in the great expanse of the harbour.

Even in the morning the heat was oppressive. Mark wore shorts and shirts or T-shirts, and Anabelle followed suit. He launched the runabout, lowering it noisily on its hydraulic crane until it splashed gently into the water. Anabelle waited apprehensively on the afterdeck, not relishing the thought of stepping from a secure stern ladder to a lurching boat.

She needn't have worried. Mark climbed down first and, as she descended after him, he gripped her firmly round the waist and hoisted her inelegantly into the launch. It rocked erratically for a few seconds, but he tightened his arms around her and she felt safe in their strength.

He widened his stance to steady the rocking motion of the small boat. The movement made her aware of how intimately close their bodies were. She took in mingled aromas of freshly laundered cotton and masculinity, and grew hot. She strained away from him and he released her as the boat stabilised. When he spoke his voice was rough.

"Sit in the front, Anabelle. I'll start the outboard."

They motored slowly towards the quay.

Ali was waiting to meet them, sitting casually on a coil of rope in the bright, glaring sun. Anabelle had noticed her well before she realised she was Ali. She stood out like a Christmas Poinsettia in a bright red flying-suit. It was impossible to miss her. She had dark hair and eyes. Her long eyelashes and delicately curved eyebrows were black and her skin an olive shade. She looked like a Latin yet she spoke with an American accent. When she stood up, she was tall and even more striking.

She greeted Mark warmly; Anabelle less so, and went on to talk about supplies and spares, names and dates. There were, clearly, many things she wanted to discuss with Mark, and Anabelle felt superfluous. She stood around wishing she'd brought

144

a sun-hat. Eventually they were joined by Johannes.

He drove up in a white Range Rover with the words 'Dalgetti Marine' painted in blue on each side. The back was filled with boxes of stores for them to load into the runabout. Johannes sprang out of the driving-seat and hailed them cheerily. He was a blond giant in jeans, T-shirt and peaked yachting cap. Anabelle guessed him to be in his thirties, but it was difficult to say. His deeply-tanned face was weather-beaten and lined, yet he was lithe and full of energy. The front of his hair and his eyebrows were bleached almost white by the sun, and he had pale, pale blue eyes.

When Johannes was introduced to Anabelle, he gave her an appraising glance and said, "So this is the lady who caused the delay." Nevertheless, he shook her hand firmly and Anabelle found his guttural Dutch accent attractive.

He backed the Range Rover up to the quayside and they loaded the supplies into the runabout. It was hot work and, to her dismay, Anabelle saw the skin of her arms and legs start to redden. She sat down for a moment on the coil of rope to apply some more lotion. Ali was checking a list while Mark passed the boxes down to Johannes in the boat. The next thing she knew, Johannes' large peaked cap had been dropped on her head.

Mark pulled her to her feet and bustled her to the shade of a nearby palm tree.

"Wait there," he ordered, adding firmly, "And I mean—don't *move*!"

A few minutes later, he returned with a cold can of drink and a wide-brimmed straw hat.

"You'd better stay there until we're loaded," Mark advised. "You're not built for these temperatures, are you?"

"No," she agreed with a short laugh. "I need time to get used to it."

Anabelle peeped in her mirror when he'd gone. Her nose and cheeks were as red as her arms. They all agreed she should stay in the shade for the rest of the day. So, after they had chugged back to *Dalgetti III* with the boxes of stores, it was decided that Ali and Anabelle would stay on board while Mark and Johannes returned to shore to collect some spares.

Ali and Anabelle unpacked the boxes in the galley.

"Thanks for the loan of the sun-screen," Anabelle remarked.

Ali shrugged. "It's not strong enough anyway." She tore open a carton. "Try this. Mark asked me to get you some." She handed Anabelle a bottle of lotion designed for fair skin.

"That's very kind of you to bother. Thanks."

Ali shrugged again. "You're Rupert Cavendish's granddaughter, aren't you."

Anabelle nodded warily.

"Lucky girl," Ali commented.

"That's a matter of opinion."

Ali laughed. "Yes, he is a crusty old devil. But, I suppose if you're as rich as he is, you can afford to be."

Anabelle didn't agree. She stacked the salad in the fridge and didn't answer.

"Why be modest about it?" Ali queried. "There's nothing like a bit of dough for smoothing out life's little wrinkles."

Anabelle thought just the opposite. It seemed to be causing more problems than it solved at the moment.

She said, "I wouldn't know, I've never had much."

"But you soon will have."

"Good heavens! What on earth makes you say that?" she asked in surprise.

"Hey, come on! It's public knowledge Rupert Cavendish is loaded. Mark wouldn't have gone to all this trouble if he hadn't thought—" Ali stopped suddenly. "I guess I've said too much. It's none of my business."

What had Mark thought? Anabelle wondered. "I didn't ask Mark to go to all this trouble," she responded stiffly. "I'm sorry if I've caused a lot of extra work."

"It's what we're paid for," Ali returned sharply. "I don't understand why he waited in England. He could have sailed much earlier and *I* could have stayed behind to escort you to Ischia by air, if he was so worried."

"Good heavens!" exploded Anabelle. "I don't need escorting. I'm not a child!"

"No, but you are Rupert Cavendish's granddaughter."

Anabelle wanted to stamp her feet and cry, "No, I'm not, I'm Anabelle Todd. I'm me!" But what was the use? She sighed irritably and suggested they start preparing lunch.

The party that evening was small and select: about a dozen French and Italian guests, all with some sea or sailing connection. Ali had arranged for a professional team to come aboard and cope with the food and drink, leaving them free to relax and enjoy the company.

A buffet was laid out in the saloon. Crabs and mussels, quiches, pâtés and cheeses were offered with abundant salads dressed with herbs and olives. They drank fruity young red wine tasting of the sun.

Johannes set up stereo speakers on the afterdeck and selected tapes so that they could dance. The night air was balmy and the sky black velvet spangled by the stars.

They dressed casually; cotton jeans and shirts or T-shirts for coolness. Anabelle chose a lilac cotton skirt and matching scoopneck T-shirt. She had curled her hair and it tumbled and shone on her shoulders.

Ali wore tight white jeans and a brief camisole top which showed off her well-kept even tan to advantage. Her long straight hair was coiled gipsy-style on the back of her head. In contrast, Mark was dressed in black lightweight trousers and a black cotton shirt.

When Mark and Ali danced together, the presented a devastatingly attractive combination. Ali snaked her arms around Mark's neck and rested her cheek against his chest as they moved sinuously to the music.

Johannes noticed Anabelle watching them and grabbed her hand, saying, "Come on. Let's dance."

He was a large man and he enveloped her with his muscular arms, holding her body close to his. She was stifled and tried to wriggle free, but Johannes just grinned and held her more tightly. Eventually, she pushed him away complaining of the heat and her tender sunburned skin. He accepted her gentle rejection and they continued to dance in a more relaxed manner. But, over his shoulder, she saw Mark stop and take Ali to a group of guests leaning on the deck rails chatting and drinking. Then he walked across to Johannes and tapped him on the shoulder.

"May I be allowed to dance with my lovely charge?" Mark asked lightly.

"I'd rather not give her up so soon, unless you insist?" Joahnnes grinned.

"I do."

Johannes dropped his arms abruptly. "Excuse me, Anabelle. I'll just go and check the tapes." He walked away quickly.

"That was a little imperious, wasn't it?" Anabelle suggested as Mark took her firmly in his arms.

He smiled and asked her if she was enjoying herself.

"Yes, I am," she answered truthfully.

"Good." Mark seemed satisfied.

He didn't hold her closely as he had done Ali, yet his hands felt like firebrands on her and she was acutely aware of every movement of his body. She held herself rigid to prevent her limbs from trembling in response, and her pulse began to quicken.

Mark twisted her tumbled curls through his fingers and murmured, "You ought to let your hair down more often, Anabelle.

You've been far too stiff and starchy these last few days."

"I've had a lot on my mind," she mumbled.

"Yes, I understand. I, too, have been preoccupied—with *Dalgetti III*." He paused and drew her closer. She resisted but he brooked no refusal and she found the steel strength of his arms too much. "My commitment to her will soon be over," he went on. "As soon as the Press coverage is complete, I'll have more free time." He turned his piercing eyes to hers. "I'd like to show you some of Ischia."

"I don't expect I shall stay very long," Anabelle replied.

"Don't you?" He smiled as though he knew something she didn't and added casually, "I think your grandfather has other ideas."

Anabelle was tempted to challenge him, but she resisted, not wanting to inflame the situation further. She smiled and said lightly, "Let's not spoil the party by going over all that again."

He regarded her shrewdly. "What a wise little girl you're turning out to be," he said.

"Don't patronise me, Mark," she hissed. "I'm not a little girl!"

"Yes, I know," he whispered. "I've known that for a long time."

His arms were around her, pressing her to him intimately.

Anabelle's heart beat so loudly that it seemed to close her throat and deafen her. Surely he could hear it? He steered her expertly to the shadows, away from the others until she felt the deck rails hard against her back. He imprisoned her with his body, smothering any protestations by gentle fingers on her lips, tracing their shape. Deftly, his hands moved sensuously to her silky hair. He seemed fascinated by the softness and the waves. His eyes glowed in the warm darkness as he caressed and twisted the curls.

The sea slapped wistfully on the hull and Anabelle's face burned; not from the sunburn she had sustained earlier, but from the mute message of Mark's movements. He was aroused and so was she. Her body ached for his and she could do nothing to assuage the pain. She guessed he knew, and maybe suffered the same, for his face was a mask of desire.

"Don't." the word was forced from her throat in a hoarse whisper.

"We can't ignore it, Anabelle," he muttered raggedly. "The attraction's there between us. Your need, my need, it's just a question of time—"

"No—" she interrupted. Her denial was lost in a babble of laughter from the guests. The music had stopped and coffee was being issued. Soon they would be leaving in the small powerboats which had brought them.

A young French couple, who made their living by chartering sailing yachts to holidaymakers, drew Mark and Anabelle back into the party to join in the joke. Another couple who ran a riding school a few miles inland had to leave as their three young children had been left with a baby-sitter, and the party began to break up.

In the mêlée of departures, Anabelle realised that Ali and Mark were also preparing to go ashore.

"I thought you'd be staying on board with us," she remarked to Ali as Mark cast off the last of the party guests.

Ali looked cool in her white camisole top

with her hair coiled smoothly out of the way. She smiled winsomely and said, "There are one or two things to see to on land before we go on to Monte Carlo. Mark's taking me back to my hotel for tonight as I'm catching an early flight in the morning."

Anabelle thought she caught a gleam of something akin to triumph in Ali's bright eyes. But perhaps it was the wine. They had all drunk plenty, to be sure.

"Mark's very understanding of my needs," Ali continued ambiguously. She smiled again. "He's a very considerate man, don't you think?"

"Oh, yes. Of course," Anabelle mumbled automatically. What was Ali trying to tell her? That she was more than just a personal assistant to Mark? That they had a relationship which was being jeopardised by Anabelle's presence?

"It's nothing to do with me what Mark gets up to with his girl friends!" Anabelle told herself fiercely. Then why did a feeling of tightness in her chest and throat overtake her as she watched Johannes cast off the runabout with them aboard? She listened to the outboard chug quietly towards the glittery shorelights, winking mockingly through the darkness.

She deliberately turned away and occupied herself tidying cushions and collecting coffee cups. The caterers had left the galley spotless. She emptied the coffee-maker and washed-up the cups. Johannes breezed in as she was putting them in the cupboard. He slapped her playfully on the bottom.

"Hi! I thought you'd gone to bed. Feel like a drink?"

"No thanks, I'll—" she began, then stopped and changed her mind. This was a party, after all! "Yes," she said decisively. "Yes, I do." She followed him into the saloon.

"I don't know about you," Johannes remarked as he headed for the sideboard, "but we needed that break. We've all been working like slaves to get this Dalgetti project launched."

"You seem to make a good team. Is it going well?"

"Well, it was. We could have done without this last hitch."

"What's that? Nothing serious, I hope."

He twisted sharply and frowned in

disbelief at her. "Are you kidding? I'm talking about you, *ma petite*."

"Me? I don't understand."

Joahnnes explained patiently. "There was no need for Mark to send us off from England like he did. Ali and I were looking forward to the trip round. But Mark insisted on delaying the date we were due to sail. I thought he was crazy. There was no reason why I couldn't have left with *Dalgetti III* on time. Mark could have stayed behind for you, if it was so important, and flown on afterwards. But no. Instead, he sent Ali and I off to rearrange things and decided to wait for you alone."

"But I was quite prepared to fly out anyway!" Anabelle interjected.

"Don't say that to Ali. She was furious, believe me."

"I'm sorry. I didn't realise."

"Don't worry about it. He'll win her round, I expect. He always does." Johannes waved an arm dismissively. "Let's forget them, shall we? Now, what do you want to drink?"

Anabelle wasn't listening. She was wondering why Mark Dalgetti would go to all that trouble to bring her personally to her grandfather. What was in it for him? She'd have to know. She'd have to ask him. Tonight. "Will he be long?" she asked.

Again Johannes regarded her in disbelief; this time mingled with contempt. "What do you think? Use your imagination, girl."

"Oh!" Anabelle blushed. It hadn't occurred to her they might actually be lovers. "I—I really didn't know they were—" she stammered.

Johannes laughed as he clinked ice into glasses. "Well, I don't know for sure, but Ali's doing all the running and Mark isn't one to look a gift horse in the mouth—" He stopped suddenly and turned. "Hey, have you and Mark got something going between you?"

"No. Certainly not!" she denied hotly.

"OK, OK," he soothed. "I simply asked. Though, the way you were looking at the pair of them dancing earlier, I did wonder then if—"

"Well, you were wrong," she broke in sharply. "There's nothing between us. Absolutely nothing."

"You seem very sure about that."

"I am."

He shrugged. "I believe you. Here, sit down and try this." He handed her a tall, straight-sided glass. It was almost filled to the brim with ice, around which trickled a pale amber fluid. "This," Johannes declared, "is the best cocktail there is."

Anabelle cautiously sipped it. It was very cold and quite sweet and didn't taste very alcoholic. She drank some more.

"Not too fast," he warned. "It's stronger than you think."

They sat in the dimly-lit saloon and Johannes was very entertaining. He made her laugh with his tales and shocked her with his escapades. He sat opposite her until he brought the second cocktail, and then he sat next to her.

Anabelle wasn't sure when the atmosphere changed, but, suddenly, he was very close to her and his arm was around her shoulders, squeezing her towards him.

"None of that." She giggled, a little under the influence of the drink. "We haven't finished tidying up yet."

"Later, my lovely," he murmured, rolling his eyes hilariously.

She laughed. "No, now."

"Yes, now," he replied, placing a hand on her waist and, although he grinned, she knew he was serious in his intentions.

"Can I kiss you?" he ventured wickedly.

"No!" she cried, twisting out of his grip.

He was a large, heavy man who used his weight to advantage. He pushed her back on to the long bench seat, and held her there firmly. She wriggled and giggled even more, losing her sandals in the process. Johannes smiled broadly, obviously enjoying himself immensely at her expense. He held her down with ease.

"Do you still say no?" he challenged playfully.

"Yes!" she yelled at the top of her voice.

"What's going on in here?"

Mark Dalgetti strode into the saloon and snapped on all the lights. Johannes got to his feet, surprised. Anabelle sat up, shading her eyes against the glare. Mark picked up a couple of cushions from the floor and replaced them on the bench seat. Then, he noticed the two cocktail glasses. He took one, sniffed at it and threw a significant glance at Johannes. He addressed Anabelle.

"I want to talk to you. In private." He paused. "Johannes, go and check the engine-room. We want to make an early start tomorrow."

When Johannes had left them, he turned again to Anabelle. "In my suite," he ordered.

"What's wrong with here?" she countered.

"I said I wanted privacy. Total privacy. Now, in my suite."

The owner's suite was on deck level in the bow. He had shown it to her previously and she had been impressed. It was more like the stateroom she had imagined would be on board a motor yacht in the luxury class: wood panelled walls and large curtained windows, not port-holes. There was a big double bed, a sitting area and also a desk. The desk was stacked around with papers and files.

"Sit down," Mark directed abruptly. "Now, what was all that about?"

"Nothing." She shrugged. "It was a bit of fun, that's all. I was enjoying myself."

She looked up at him, towering over her. "Isn't that what you want me to do?" she enquired with false innocence.

"Stay away from Johannes. We've got a busy schedule to keep and I don't want you distracting him from his work."

"Well! Of all the nerve!" She stood up to challenge him. "We were having a drink together. That's allowed, isn't it?"

"A drink, was it? Do you usually behave like that with a man you've only just met?"

"Behave like what?" she retaliated, astounded by his attitude. "It was quite harmless! The only thing he did was ask for a kiss, and I said 'no'!"

"It sounded like 'yes' to me."

Anabelle's irritation snapped. "I don't see why I should have to explain my actions to you." She flashed her grey eyes at him angrily. "If I want to kiss him, I shall."

"No, you will not!" he seethed.

"Oh no?" she returned archly. "How will you stop me?" "This is getting worse," she thought. "Who does he think he is?" She drew herself up to her full height and added sweetly, "At least he had the decency to ask me first. That's more than you did."

"Then he's a fool!"

Mark gripped her arms roughly and dragged her towards him. He kissed her harshly, his mouth hard and cruel on hers, and her head reeled with the speed of his actions. He hurt her and that made her hate him. For, while her palms itched to wind through his hair and her traitorous body yearned to be close to his, she was painfully aware that this kiss was one of anger.

Where she found the strength, she didn't know, but her instinct for self-preservation was keen and she stayed impassive, without response; a block of ice. Of course, he realised and momentarily released the pressure on her. In that instant when his lips left hers and he frowned, puzzled, searching her eyes for the truth, she snapped, "Haven't you worked all that off with Ali?"

It was unforgivable, she knew. In the ensuing tense moments, she thought that he would strike her. Bravely, she held his gaze and saw his eyes turn cold as glass;

cold green glass. His lips compressed into a thin hard line and his head moved very slightly from side to side, indicating a negation. Of what? Of her accusation? Or of her?

He let her go, moving away as though she were contaminated, and retaliated, "That acid tongue of yours will be your downfall."

"Or yours," she bit back sharply.

They stared at each other in mutual acrimony, then Anabelle sighed irritably. They were on the road to nowhere. This wasn't the way to get answers to her questions. She swung round, dragging her fingers through her already dishevelled hair.

"Why, Mark? Why did you engineer this trip so that we'd be alone?" She waited in the silence for his reply.

"I think you know the answer to that by now," he said.

"Do I?"

"What do you want me to say?" he exploded. "That you're an attractive, spirited woman and I want you in my bed?"

Anabelle choked back a cry. Just like that! A convenient diversion for him. She felt as if she'd been punched in the stomach.

"Is it true?" she whispered.

"Yes."

"And is that the only reason?"

"No. I wanted to know more about you —the real you—before you and Rupert confronted each other." She heard him laugh harshly. "It seemed a good idea at the time. But I reckoned without your Cavendish pride and obstinacy."

"I've told you, I'm not a Cavendish!"

"You are, you know," he returned levelly. "Very much so."

Anabelle whirled back to face him. "And you're not!" she cried emphatically. "So why are you so involved?"

"My family owe a lot to Rupert Cavendish. He once saved my father from bankruptcy and they were business partners until my father died. I have a great respect for your grandfather. Most of what I know about commerce and finance I've learned from him. He treated me as though I were his own son before I established my own company." He stopped, aware of the pain he might be causing her. "I didn't know he'd had a son," Mark continued by way of explanation. "He never talked of Paul."

Anabelle frowned. "But the painting—you were at the auction?"

"I didn't find out about Paul—or his work—until after your grandfather's recent heart attack. He already suffered from arthritis and his illness made him reassess his life. He had to give up many of his business interests. He sold up his villa and moved permanently into one of the spa hotels on Ischia, with his daughter Eleanor. But he took with him his collection of paintings—Paul Cavendish paintings." Mark frowned as though it was difficult for him to go on.

"Then he talked of his son. Yet—never mentioned his marriage." He shrugged restlessly. "The end of the story, you know. I travel widely in connection with my boat building enterprises and offered to look out for other Paul Cavendish works." He narrowed his eyes and regarded her keenly. "When I came across you, after the same painting, I was sceptical of your claims, to say the least. Then Rupert told me about Paul's marriage,

166

about you, the car crash and—and—Joanna."

"Did he tell you how abominably he treated my mother?" she demanded.

"He had his reasons! You know that as well as I do!"

"Oh, yes! Jealousy! Paul loved her in preference to him!"

"It was more than that! Damn you, Anabelle, she was responsible for Paul's death!"

"What?" Anabelle's mouth dropped open incredulously.

"She was lucky not to be charged and convicted!" he added.

"Liar!" Instinctively, Anabelle raised her right arm and aimed a blow from the back of her hand across his face.

But he was quicker than she and his steely fingers grasped her wrist, holding her off, twisting her arm until it hurt.

"Don't you ever try anything like that again!" he seethed through clenched teeth.

"You asked for it by suggesting such foul things," she cried. Her arm was aching, straining against his superior strength, locked in combat.

"Suggesting? It's the truth, Anabelle. She was driving and she was drunk."

Anabelle wrenched at her arm, trying unsuccessfully to free it. "No!" she denied. "That's a lie!"

"That is fact," he replied firmly.

He said it with such conviction that she was momentarily stunned. She relaxed her arm, and he lowered it carefully, placing it where it belonged, safely by her side. She was shaking her head unconsciously, silently mouthing the word 'no' over and over again.

"I'm sorry," Mark murmured. He sounded contrite, sympathetic. "I didn't realise that you didn't know."

"I don't believe it." Anabelle's voice was quiet.

"It's true. As I understand it, there was some talk of causing death by dangerous driving. But the charge was dropped, thanks to your grandfather's well-paid lawyers. So, you see, Anabelle, he thought Joanna was trouble. And he had your interests at heart when he asked her to give you up."

"Joanna? Trouble?" Anabelle was whispering half to herself. "It doesn't make sense." She raised her voice. "You've met her, Mark. Do you believe it?"

"I admit I was surprised. Pleasantly so. She's a fine woman."

Anabelle felt weak. She glanced around hastily and sat on the nearest chair.

"We all make mistakes sometimes; Joanna, you, I," Mark began softly.

"Even Rupert Cavendish?" Anabelle interrupted.

"Even Rupert Cavendish." Mark ran his fingers through his unruly black hair. "Meeting him isn't going to be easy, Anabelle—for either of you." He stared at her thoughtfully for a long time. "I think the biggest mistake is mine. I persuaded him to invite you. A reconciliation was my idea. I set it up."

She sighed heavily. "At least I have a few more days to adjust, but I can't honestly say I'm looking forward to it."

She gazed at her bare toes and lapsed into silence. She heard him move towards her. She heard the rustle of his shirt, then he took her hands and drew her to her feet. She felt the magnetism between them, drawing them together, a strong invisible force. "I want to be in his arms," she thought, "to hold him and be held by him. That's what I want. And I've never felt like this about any man before. Oh, what's happening to me?"

She shook off his sensuous touch on her fingers and lifted her head, steeling herself to ignore the desire in his eyes and the longings of her own treacherous body.

"Good night, Mark," she said clearly and walked steadily to the door.

He didn't reply and she didn't look back. She didn't realise, until she reached her own cabin, that she'd been holding her breath and also, that she'd been willing him to come after her. But he didn't.

7

MONTE CARLO!
They slipped quietly into the sheltered harbour after dark. Ali came on board early the next day, bringing with her the specially ordered crew's kit they planned to wear for the Press conference. The sea was placid and a veil of mist shrouded the upperlayers of the town. White and cream buildings crowded, tier upon tier, away from the shore until they disappeared with the Monaco hills into the heat haze.

On the water, *Dalgetti III* was easily outshone by the collection of opulent sea craft already moored there. Huge cruisers, floating hotels, dominated the deep water berths of the port. They were the limousines of the sea. And, if that was true, then *Dalgetti III* was the sports model; smaller, more compact, but packing a punch. She had a lot going for her, Mark pointed out, and Anabelle had to agree. She was drawn into his enthusiasm for the yacht and hoped it would be a success.

Ali and Johannes, too, were infected by the excitement of presenting the *Dalgetti III* at her very best to the reporters and photographers. All four of them tidied, dusted, scrubbed and polished until every corner sparkled.

Mark and Ali had some paperwork to complete. It seemed to Anabelle that Ali spent much of her time by Mark's right elbow, whether he needed her or not. He didn't mind, she guessed. Ali was a good-looking woman and Mark Dalgetti liked beautiful women as much as he liked beautiful boats. It would be sheer madness to allow herself to become involved with such a man.

In contrast, Anabelle had the distinct impression that Johannes was being deliberately off-hand with her. Several times he was brusque when she chatted to him, implying he had a lot of work to do and was busy.

She wondered if he'd been warned off her by Mark—as she had been him—after the party. If so, it annoyed her, but she accepted it. She didn't want to stir up trouble. It appeared that Mark Dalgetti could be a hard taskmaster when the occasion demanded it.

Just before the Press were due, they unpacked the crew's kit to choose their own selection to wear. And what a choice! Cotton trousers and shorts in brilliant white and nautical blue, long and short sleeved T-shirts, and comfortable sweat-shirts in matching colours, all with the name of the yacht printed boldly across the front. It was a uniform. Whatever each of them chose, they would look as though they belonged together and to the *Dalgetti III*.

At times Anabelle felt a bit superfluous. She didn't speak the language and knew even less about sailing. But that didn't stop the photographers taking her photo-graph. Her skin was beginning to turn brown and her golden hair had lighter, sunbleached streaks at the frnt. When she looked in the mirror, her grey eyes shone back at her with a healthy glow.

However, it was exhausting for the others. To be constantly on show and at the mercy of a barrage of questions was quite a strain. She marvelled at how well

Mark weathered it; how he seemed to thrive on the challenge.

They went ashore that evening to celebrate. Mark stood them all a wildly extravagant dinner in a very expensive hotel. Dressed in their *Dalgetti III* uniforms, they drank champagne and ate lobster.

The atmosphere was happy and relaxed. All differences between any of them evaporated and were forgotten. They returned to the yacht tired but in good spirits. *Dalgetti III* was due to sail for Ischia the following day.

As the Monaco hills receded in the bright sun of the next morning, Mark, Ali and Johannes prepared for a similar day of Press invasion when they reached Naples. Anabelle's thoughts turned to her mother.

She leaned over the railings on the afterdeck, watching the turbulent dark water being churned white by powerful twin propellers. Had Joanna really been responsible for her father's death? Was that the reason she never spoke of the accident? Had it become too great a burden to bear, so that she preferred to forget all about it?

Twice, Anabelle had been on the point of ringing Joanna, using the radio phone in the wheelhouse. She hesitated because she felt that if there was some dark secret concerning the accident, Joanna would have told her, if she had wanted her to know. And if she didn't want her to know, then Anabelle didn't want to know either.

She didn't hear Mark's soft footsteps on the deck. She hadn't realised he was there until he rested his elbows on the rails and stared at the water with her.

"Thinking about tomorrow?" he queried.

She nodded.

"Are you nervous of meeting your grandfather?"

"No. Oh, I don't know."

"Then you are."

"Wouldn't you be?" she said defensively, turning to look at him. He was wearing shorts and a T-shirt, as she was, in pristine white to show off his rapidly deepening tan. Even in casual clothes, he gave the impression of being capable and in full control of events. She added as an afterthought, "No, I suppose you wouldn't." She sighed. "I didn't mean to snap. I guess I'm a bit uptight about things."

"And rightly so. It must have been quite a shock for you, to find out about the accident from—from me. I'm sorry."

"Yes, it was a shock," Anabelle thought. "But not because I had no knowledge of it before. I simply don't believe it. There's been some mistake—or some deliberate lie."

When she didn't comment aloud, Mark continued. "Still, whatever the differences are between Rupert and Joanna, I know he doesn't hold anything against you, Anabelle."

"That's noble of him!" she replied drily.

"Don't be cynical! You're all he's got."

"There's Eleanor—my aunt Eleanor," Anabelle pointed out.

"An introverted middle-aged spinster who's spent her life in her father's shadow? He's quite open about the fact that she's a disappointment to him. It's not surprising she's bitter sometimes."

"Is she? Bitter, I mean."

Mark twisted his mouth in thought. "I think so. If anyone is going to be difficult, it will be her. She may not welcome your visit at all. But Rupert will, I know. Give him a chance, Anabelle. After all those lost years, you owe him one chance."

"Do I?" She did sound cynical. She could hear it herself.

"Yes."

"All right, all right. I'm here, aren't I? I'm trying. Though there's one issue I won't compromise on, Mark. He can't take me into his fold alone. He must accept Joanna as well."

"I think that's too much to ask of him."

"And without that acceptance, it's too much to ask of me! You must see that!"

He was silent for a moment. When he spoke, his voice sounded gruff and strained, as if he were angry with her for some reason.

Or with himself? "I'll take you ashore tomorrow and stay until you're settled."

"Oh, that's not necessary," she said wearily. "I'll behave myself, I promise. Besides, you've got to go to Naples with the others, haven't you?"

"Don't argue!" he snapped. "I'm responsible for bringing you here and, whatever you think of my motives, I am

177

concerned about a reconciliation between you and your grandfather."

He sounded so angry that Anabelle wondered for a moment if he regretted his actions from the beginning. Well, she thought, that was between him and his own conscience. She wasn't sure what agreement had been made with her grandfather by him, and she didn't really want to find out. Mark's part in the deal would soon be finished. As soon as she was with her grandfather, they need never see each other again.

The realisation disturbed her. She didn't like the idea of never seeing him again. He had swung round andwas leaning with his back to the deck rails. His face was grim, the skin taut over his jutting jaw. His expression reminded her of their disagreements. He could be so infuriating at times! Yet, for all their differences, she would miss him when he was gone.

"Mark, I—" she began.

"Yes?"

"I know we haven't always seen eye to eye over some things, but, well, thanks for—"

"Thanks? For what?" he interrupted.

"For turning your life upside-down? I should have left you behind in England, happily selling your books"

He's still angry, she thought. Why?

"It was my decision," she argued. "I wouldn't have come if I hadn't been prepared to face the consequences. I knew what I was doing."

"Did you?"

"Yes." Now, it was her turn to be firm.

She watched his features relax and his shoulders sag. "Yes," he agreed with a sigh. "You're very much a woman of today, aren't you? Intelligent. Independent." He turned suddenly and smiled at her. His even teeth flashed white against his darkening tan, causing a strange exhilaration to run through her. She blinked, startled by the change in his mood.

"Is that meant to be a compliment?" she asked lightly.

"Yes."

The gleam in his eyes sent a thrill of anticipation down her back. Anticipation? Of what? She levered herself from the deck rails and moved away, murmuring, "Thank you."

His hand gripped like a vice on her

wrist. It surprised her. She hadn't intended leaving, only putting a little distance between them. Safe distance. But he had other ideas and he drew her back.

She trembled at his nearness. She could not control it. He did this to her every time he was close and, as he released his hold on her, he smiled—a secretive smile, as if he knew.

She didn't move. She didn't want to fight him. She wanted to stay friends. Could she make light of the life force that was drawing them inexorably together with each passing second?

"Let's part as friends," she suggested evenly. It took a lot of effort and, although her voice was steady, her lips quivered as she spoke.

He raised a straight black eyebrow. "Friends?" he queried softly. "Is that what we are?"

His movements were unhurried. He seemed to know she could not shift. Her feet were rooted to the deck, her body rigid with expectation.

His eyes shone like polished jade, piercing her defences. He regarded her seriously, his head to one side, and carefully, gently, set her hair behind her shoulders, smoothing it from her face. Then he grasped her upper arms and bent his head to touch his lips on her forehead.

"That's a friendly kiss, Anabelle," he whispered, trailing his sensitive mouth down her cheek to her ear.

Her skin was on fire. It tingled as he teased her emotions. His smooth clean jaw, smelling of soap, was on hers. Skilful lips nibbled her earlobe and blushing neck. She closed her eyes and allowed the heady sensation of his light, feathery kisses to flow over her.

As he continued his tantalising search for a response, her frozen stance melted and softened in his enveloping arms. When he sensed her compliance, his mouth moved to hers, insistently demanding more from her.

His kisses inflamed her passion as never before. Her heart beat faster, her pulse raced.

He raised his head and pressed his hands on her back, holding her tightly, as though afraid to let her go. She could hear the fast thud of his heart and smell the cotton of his T-shirt.

"Is this how friends behave?" he said quietly. His voice was rough and strained.

Anabelle's throat was closed, her senses shattered, shaken to the core by the strength of her own longing. She pushed away, confused. He didn't stop her.

"I—I—" It was no good. She couldn't formulate her thoughts, let alone any words to express them. She looked away.

A movement caught her eye. A shadow moved across the saloon. It must be Ali. It was too dark to see, but it had to be; Johannes was in the wheelhouse. She heard the galley door slam shut. It brought her back to reality.

Mark, too, seemed to jerk to his senses, though his face was flushed and his eyes glittered through their thick black lashes.His eyes narrowed and he frowned. Did he regret his actions? Did she? Anabelle pressed her palms against her heated face as if to conceal the outward signs of her desire. Yet, she couldn't deny it. So she did not even try to.

She had to escape, before she made a complete fool of herself. She struggled to find her voice. "I—I have to go and pack," she managed inanely.

He shrugged, continued to watch her closely, but didn't reply. Instead, he stepped back, allowing her to pass, and she walked unsteadily across the deck to the welcome dimness of the saloon.

They reached Ischia the following day. *Dalgetti III* anchored a little way off shore from the landing stage beneath Mark's villa. He was to take her ashore as promised, and drive her to the hotel that was now her grandfather's permanent home. They were both expected for lunch.

As the runabout was launched, Anabelle waited on the afterdeck with her suitcase. The island was greener than she'd imagined. She'd assumed, as it was southern Italy, that it would be more arid; dry and rocky. But the thickly wooded slopes in front of her were luxuriantly green.

She remarked on this to Mark when they were chugging slowly to a wooden jetty at the foot of the hillside.

"*Isola Verde*," he explained. "'Green Island'. Ischia's origins are volcanic, so the

183

soil is extremely fertile. The slopes of the volcano are covered with the most luscious vineyards and citrus groves."

Anabelle's eyebrows shot up. "Volcano? It's not still active, is it?"

"No." He laughed. "Mount Epomeo has been quiet for six or seven hundred years now."

"Have you always lived here?"

He shook his head. "It was a holiday home at first. After my father died, my mother remarried quickly and went to live in the States. I sold the house in Naples and moved here."

They were approaching the landing stage. She watched him silently for a moment, standing at the wheel of the small motor-boat. The breeze ruffled his wild hair further, as he manoeuvred the small craft carefully into position. He tied up beside the only other boat there; a larger power-boat with its outboard engine shrouded inside a plastic cover. The name painted on its sleek pointed bow was *Alison*.

Alison? Ali? she wondered. Anabelle reflected on Mark's relationship with Ali as they clambered out of the boat. They spent a lot of time together. But then, of course, they would. She worked for him. Was it just a professional association, or was there more? They were certainly very familiar with each other at times.

Ali had hinted at something more when Mark had taken her ashore after the party in Montpellier. And Johannes had supported that view, but said he wasn't sure. She'd pushed it from her mind then, telling herself it was none of her business and anyway, she didn't care! But she did. She cared then, and she cared now.

He'd heaved her suitcase on to the jetty and then offered her his hand to climb ashore. He'd changed into light beige cords and a toning open-necked cotton shirt. Anabelle, too, was more formally dressed in a neat shirtwaister of muted pastel shades.

Their eyes met briefly as their fingers entwined. Anabelle urged herself to control the involuntary shiver that passed through her when they touched. His expression was very steady, unfathomable, as she scrambled up beside him.

"Thanks," she said, slightly breathless.

"Nervous?" he asked.

She nodded.

"Don't be, he's only human."

Mark was referring to her grandfather, she knew, and she smiled weakly in agreement.

Trees grew thickly, right down to the water's edge, and a stepped path wound through them to the villa. It was a steep climb, which they took slowly. Before they reached the house, the woodland fell away to reveal a large paved area containing an oval swimming-pool. The water glinted, cool and inviting, in the hot sun. They continued up a curved stone staircase to a wide terrace fronting the villa. Mark dropped her suitcase on the tiles and unlocked the French doors into the house.

"Would you like a drink to calm the butterflies?" he asked.

"No, thanks. I'd rather keep a clear head."

"OK." He shrugged. He waved-an arm expansively. "This is where I live. Your grandfather has booked you a room in his hotel, but—" he hesitated and grimaced— "if you do find things too difficult to handle, you're welcome to stay here."

"That's very kind of you, though I don't expect I shall stay long, whatever happens. Thanks for the offer."

He shrugged again. "Well, it's here if you want it. A couple from the village keep an eye on it for me while I'm away. They always know where to find me."

His car was kept at the back of the house, which was the side away from the sea. She followed him through light, airy rooms with ceramic floors, rugs and cane furniture. A robust Citroën saloon stood in the shade of a carport among the shrubs. The engine fired into life on the second attempt and he drove up a steep winding drive to the main coast road.

It was a beautiful island, with pines and palms sweeping down to sandy beaches, and terraces of vines and fruit scaling the hill slopes. Mark told her of its reputation as a spa resort. Numerous thermal springs gave Ischia a worldwide reputation for curing many ailments and it was fondly called, by some, the "Island of Eternal Youth".

Rupert Cavendish's hotel was situated in one of the spa centres. It was a modern building, near to the natural springs, built to cope with the increasing popularity of the cures. The receptionist directed them to the wide patio outside the dining-room.

Her grandfather rose to greet her, leaning heavily on his stick to do so. His white hair was sparse and his blue eyes watery and faded. Anabelle was shocked to see him look so old and ill. He was emaciated and his papery skin was brown with the sallow tinge of sickness rather than a summer tan. Despite the heat, he wore a woollen cardigan around his shoulders.

Eleanor Cavendish helped her father to sit down again, then took Anabelle's offered hand briefly, hardly touching her, and certainly not shaking it as Rupert had done. Anabelle was surprised to find that she was much older than Joanna. Her grey hair was well-cut to frame her pinched, intense face. She was a thin woman, dressed in an Indian print smock and, although she smiled at Anabelle, the younger girl felt the chill of her greeting.

They lunched on the patio and the meal was good. *Fettuccine alla Marinara—* ribbon noodles in tomato sauce and fresh basil—followed by veal cutlets and salads. As they ate they talked, and Anabelle realised that, even though her grandfather was physically in poor shape, his mind was very agile and he clearly enjoyed Mark's stimulating company and conversation. In contrast, Eleanor was quiet. She hardly spoke a word, but her grey-blue eyes darted sharply about the table as the meal progressed.

Rupert Cavendish turned to Anabelle over coffee and said, "Mark tells me your mother has made a modest success of her bookshop. She has built up a sound business—and with your help, I understand."

"Yes, that's right." Anabelle nodded, glancing at Mark. He seemed unconcerned with the turn in the topic of their discussions. He continued spooning sugar into his cup.

"I didn't think she had it in her," Rupert added.

Anabelle's fingers tightened round her cup. "Why do you say that?" she queried.

"Don't misinterpret me, my dear," her grandfather countered. "It's all to her credit. She had nothing when she married my son." He paused. "Or when she was widowed either."

Anabelle replaced her cup carefully in its saucer. "I'm sure she didn't expect anything."

"No?" Her grandfather smiled, but it was a smile of irony.

"You still think she was a fortune-hunter, don't you?"

"Why not? She was a shrewd woman. For that I admire her."

Anabelle moved her hands out of sight under the table and clenched her fists. "If you believe that, I suppose you think that I'm here for exactly the same reason," she said quietly.

"Frankly, no. I would have thought that if you hadn't taken quite so much persuading to come here. Mark must be losing his touch, he doesn't usually have such problems with women."

"No, I'm sure he doesn't," Anabelle returned drily, glancing in Mark's direction for a second time. He was more attentive now. He shifted his chair slightly, moving it marginally nearer to hers. "For your information," Anabelle went on, "it wasn't Mark who persuaded me to come here. It was my mother."

"Ah," Rupert replied. "Then she does have some regrets for her past behaviour."

"Certainly not—" A hand gripped Anabelle's under the table, effectively stalling her with surprise.

"I've talked to Joanna," Mark interrupted quickly. "My impression is that what has happened in the past is over and any differences are between her and you, sir. She is proud of her daughter and happy for her to reach her own conclusions on the issues." He flashed a warm smile at Anabelle. "Would you agree with that assessment of the situation, Anabelle?"

"Y-Yes. Yes, indeed." Anabelle thought it was a very accurate grasp of her views.

Her grandfather appeared to become agitated. His hands began to shake slightly and he spoke sharply. "Even after all these years she is not repentant."

"There is nothing to repent," Anabelle retaliated stiffly.

He made an impatient gesture to Eleanor, saying, "My pills, dear. Come along, my pills."

Eleanor fumbled in her bag and

produced a bottle of capsules, while Mark poured a glass of water. Anabelle watched, silently biting her lip as Rupert swallowed them.

"It's time for your rest, Father," Eleanor said bluntly and seemingly without sympathy.

"Yes, yes," he replied tetchily. "Damn doctors. I pay them the earth to make my life a misery. Give me a hand up then, dear."

Mark was already on his feet and giving Rupert assistance, which he shook off as soon as he was standing.

Rupert addressed Anabelle. "We'll talk again tomorrow, my dear. You'll have lunch with me. Here. I take breakfast alone in my room and never eat dinner. You must lunch with me every day." He didn't wait for her answer. Anabelle understood she had no choice in the matter. "Come on, Eleanor," he continued, "give me your arm."

She obeyed silently, apparently without question.

Anabelle sank to her chair with her head in her hands, when they'd left. She wished

Mark didn't have to go back to the boat and on to Naples. He was right; this was going to be difficult.

"Oh, dear," she sighed. "Now I feel awful. I upset him on our first meeting."

"No," Mark argued emphatically. "That's just his manner. He has to keep to a strict regimen and it annoys him."

"I hope you're right. Is he really very ill?"

"Yes."

"Why didn't you tell me how seriously ill he was?"

"He insists on ignoring his illness if he can."

"It's arthritis, isn't it?" Anabelle said.

"And heart trouble. That's the main complication."

Anabelle blew out her cheeks and shook her head. "I don't think I should go through with this."

"Why not?"

"It's only going to open up old wounds! That can't be good for him, surely?"

"He wants a reconciliation. I know he does."

"And Eleanor?" Anabelle queried. "She obviously hates the sight of me!"

"That's a harsh judgment on the strength of one meeting."

"Is it?"

"They need time to get used to you. Both of them. You must stay, Anabelle. You must."

"Yes, I know, but it's not that easy!"

"You're overtired. You need rest. Tomorrow, you'll see things in a different way."

"I suppose so," she agreed grudgingly. Mark really did seem keen for her to stay. She wondered why. Perhaps he hadn't told her everything. She saw him glance surreptitiously at his watch. Or, perhaps, he simply wanted to make sure she was ensconced in the hotel so that he could get back to the boat and go on to Naples. She knew he had a tight schedule and that he had to fly to Milan some time, to see his bankers. She wanted to ask him when she'd see him again, but pride forbade her.

They walked back to the hotel reception and parted casually: she to her room and he to the car park.

She was alone and she felt it deeply. Isolated. Trapped among aliens.

When she went down to dinner, she

asked for Miss Cavendish and was told that her aunt was dining in her room. Anabelle took it as a snub and dined alone. The varied menu was wasted on her that evening. She had no appetite. She ate little, and slept badly.

The next morning she was up early and breakfasting on the patio when Aunt Eleanor joined her. The older woman was immaculate in a fresh cotton kaftan. The air was already uncomfortably warm and the day promised to be a scorcher. Anabelle realised the advantage of wearing an airy tent instead of the tight jeans she had put on that morning. She'd tied her hair back with a ribbon and she knew it didn't suit her features, but it kept it out of the way. The coffee was too bitter for her tastes and the apricot jam too sickly sweet. Anabelle felt depressed. The appearance of Eleanor made it worse.

Eleanor drew out a chair and a waiter materialised from nowhere. She gave her order in fluent Italian.

Anabelle put down her knife and asked politely, "How is my grandfather this morning?"

"Not at all well," her aunt replied. The scowl on her face emphasised the lines. If only she would smile, Anabelle thought, she wouldn't seem so resentful. Eleanor went on, "I won't have him upset by you. Your presence here disturbs him."

"I'm sorry to hear that." There was a silence while the waiter brought a fresh pot of coffee. Anabelle offered Eleanor the basket of rolls. She declined, poured herself a large cup of coffee and heaped sugar into it. Anabelle continued, "I am here at my grandfather's invitation, Aunt."

"How long did it take you to persuade him?" Eleanor demanded coldly.

"To invite me? I didn't. I assure you I—"

"Don't be coy with me. It might work with Mark, but I've seen your sort around too often; batting their eyelids to get what they want."

Anabelle widened her eyes in surprise. "You've got it wrong, Aunt Eleanor. It wasn't my idea to come out here."

"No, but it was yours to get Mark to plead your case to my father!" She stopped, then added maliciously, "What price did he ask? Or did you have some other form of payment?"

What a catty thing to say! Anabelle clenched her fist on the tablecloth. She couldn't answer that Mark had nothing to do with her decision, because he had. She kept silent and gritted her teeth.

Eleanor hadn't finished. "I suppose you cooked up the plan between you, to get your hands on the Cavendish money."

"That's the last thing I want," Anabelle denied hotly. Several other guests looked in her direction. She lowered her voice. "I don't know where you got that notion from, but it's not true. When I met Mark, I had no idea he even knew my grandfather. My only concern was to buy the portrait, so I made him an offer."

"Oh, yes. The portrait." Eleanor sounded cynical. "If that's all you want, why don't you just take it and go? My father said he'd give it to you if you came to collect it, didn't he? We certainly don't want a picture of the woman who killed my brother!"

The words cut cruelly through to Anabelle's heart. She was not in a fighting mood and tears pricked her eyelids. It was

197

a wounding lie and, while Eleanor and Rupert Cavendish believed it, there could be no grounds for any reconciliation. Her father had died in an accident, hadn't he? *An accident.* She couldn't stay amongst people who bore her mother so much malice.

Anabelle stood up. "I'm sorry you still feel so bitter about the past. I have no desire to prolong my visit if it upsets you and your father. Although I admit I do want the portrait, I didn't come for that. I came because I was persuaded it was my duty. But, clearly, I am not welcome." She paused to take a breath. Her tears were dangerously close. The older woman was unmoved. Anabelle made a final effort. "I'll make arrangements to leave immediately," she said steadily. "If you truly do not want the portrait, then my offer to buy it is still open."

Anabelle walked away from the table with her head held high. It had been a dreadful mistake to come here in the first place, she realised. Why hadn't she trusted her own instincts and defied everyone else? She crossed the patio and hurried blindly through the hotel dining-room to reception, wondering how soon she could arrange the journey home.

Her hands were shaking. She shoved them in her jeans pockets and slowed, ostensibly to look at the carousel of postcards by the desk until she regained her composure.

The man on reception was different from yesterday. She hoped he spoke some English. Her Italian was almost nonexistent beyond basic "please" and "thank you" phrases. After one false start, she said, rather loudly, "I want to leave. For England."

He appeared puzzled; not because he hadn't understood, she suspected, but because he thought she was crazy. She'd only just arrived, hadn't she?

Suddenly his face relaxed into a smile, and she heard a familiar voice behind her speaking in Italian. Mark? She spun round, surprised. What was he doing here? Yes, it was him, dressed in faded old jeans and a white cotton T-shirt that clung closely to his fine tanned torso. In spite of all her problems, a frisson of desire ran through her and she thought, I *am* attracted to him. I am.

He trained his eyes on hers. "You didn't mean what you just said, did you?"

"Yes." She shook her head emphatically. "I can't stay. It's not working and I don't belong. As soon as I've found out the plane times, I'm going to ring my mother and then go home."

"No, you're not," he stated flatly.

"There's no point in staying!" She pushed a stray lock of hair behind her ear. "Eleanor hates me. Rupert hates my mother. Nothing's changed in all these years. Nothing." She stopped. Her voice was high. She was causing a disturbance in the foyer.

Mark spoke rapidly to the man at the desk and led her away to a quiet corner. "Can't you make allowances, Anabelle? I know it's difficult. I was there yesterday, and I do have eyes and ears, you know!"

"Is that why you came back?" she retaliated irritably. "To keep me out of trouble? Shouldn't you be in Naples now, selling your yacht?"

"Yes, I should," he snapped angrily. "But, I take it I have your permission to spend a few days in my own home if I want!" He glared at her.

The sarcasm wasn't lost on her, though she was too keyed-up to be deflected. "What else should I think? I know you have a tight schedule—"

"That's my worry, not yours!" he flung back, his green eyes flashing. Then, unexpectedly, he relented. He took a deep breath and went on quietly, "This is getting precisely nowhere. Johannes and Ali can handle the publicity perfectly well without me. I trained them, so I should know—they're more than capable." His expression hardened. "That's more than I can say for you, Anabelle, at the moment. You're not handling this situation at all well. I expected better of you."

"Did you?" She returned some of his sarcasm. "'Sorry to disappoint you, *sir*. I'll try harder next time."

"Oh, dear," she thought. "Now he's mad again. Well, so am I!"

"It's Eleanor," she explained irately. "Aunt Eleanor. I've tried to ignore it, but I can't! You do know what she thinks, don't you?" Anabelle didn't give him a chance to answer. She lifted her chin and directed her clear grey eyes into his. "She thinks *I* planned this visit from the start —to get my hands on the Cavendish money. I'm surprised she didn't add 'just like your scheming mother', for that's what you all seem to think!"

She could hear her querulous tone herself in the tirade of words. Yet, it didn't sem to matter any more. The emotion poured from her.

"Do you know what she asked me?" Anabelle went on. "She asked me what price I paid you, to plead my case to Rupert! She asked me what I had to do to persuade you to bring me here!" She was ranting and she knew it, but she couldn't stop herself. She laughed hysterically, almost choking on her words. "She thinks I slept with you!" Her voice rose. "Isn't that funny? Don't you think that's funny, Mark?" She began to giggle uncontrollably.

But Mark wasn't laughing. His face was grim. "No, I don't," he replied evenly. "I think you're overwrought." His fingers curled round her arms, gripping tightly. He shook her firmly. "Calm down,

Anabelle. Eleanor's jealous of you that's all. Don't you see? She's jealous of Joanna too."

"But why?"

"Who can say for sure? She's one of life's unfortunate losers who've never found their way genuinely into anyone's affections—least of all her own father's." Mark shrugged. "And probably not her brother's either."

Anabelle quietened. Was this true? she wondered.

"She said I wasn't wanted here. She said I upset my grandfather," Anabelle muttered.

Mark sighed heavily. His shoulders sagged. "He's had a relapse. Not serious, but I assume it's connected with your arrival. It might be wiser if you don't visit him for a while."

"A long while, I should think."

"You're not leaving the island," Mark warned.

"You can't stop me," she challenged.

"Can't I? Try me."

She thought as he spoke, he grew a little —both taller and broader. He drew himself up to his full overpowering height and hooked his thumbs loosely into the waistband of his jeans. It smacked of swagger to Anabelle and she didn't like it.

"What will you do?" she queried. "Hit me over the head with a club and drag me back to your lair?" She laughed falsely to show her contempt. But his expression made her freeze, mouth half-open, and her heart missed a beat.

"Is that what you'd like, Anabelle?" he asked seriously.

He'd caught her unawares. She hadn't meant it literally, of course, yet the idea excited her, unwillingly. Not the brutal caveman aspect—but the thought of being carried away by Mark and of being physically close to him, enticed her in a way that made her slightly uneasy. She looked at him. Those green eyes were piercing hers as if they could read her thoughts.

She replied shakily. "No, of course not. I—I was joking."

"It's just as well. I'm not into violence. I'd hoped to use other ways to persuade you to stay."

"Such as?"

"Can you swim?"

She nodded warily.

"I'll take you to a rocky cove where the water is so clear you can count the pebbles on the seabed, and the fish are so tame you can feed them from your hand."

"Go on, I don't believe you!" She smiled.

"A smile! That's better. Why don't you go up to your room, pack a beach bag and enjoy a little of our beautiful island for a day? Or is one more day too much to ask of you?"

No. Of course it wasn't too much to ask of her, and she agreed. She'd acted too hastily, too emotionally, and the tension had drained her energy. A chance to recuperate and think was welcome.

They were to go to the cove by sea, and drove to Mark's villa to pick up *Alison*. She was already packed with snorkelling equipment when they reached her. Mark collected a cold box from the kitchen of his villa as they passed through. It was obvious that this trip was planned and not a spontaneous decision. For a moment, she speculated on what he would have done if she'd refused to come but. she realised immediately, he would have taken someone else. Mark Dalgetti was an attractive man and there were probably several other girls he could have asked instead. He would never be short of an escort.

When all was stowed aboard and Anabelle seated, Mark started the outboard and they set off. *Alison* was much more powerful than the runabout from *Dalgetti III* and much faster. They covered the sea miles quickly.

They skirted the wooded, rocky headland, leaving a curving, widening trail of foam in their wake. Anabelle tilted her face to the sun, delighting in the exhilarating freedom of the warm wind on her skin. They raced on until they came to a narrow strip of sand, visible at the foot of the cliffs. Mark cut the engine and they drifted gently to ground on the beach.

Rough-hewn rocks clothed in lush vegetation rose challengingly from a clear aquamarine sea and boulders formed a rugged boundary enclosing the small cove, making it a secret, private place.

Mark leapt over the side of the small craft and landed thigh-deep in the sea.

With remarkable agility and energy, he pulled the boat further up on to the sand.

"That's as far as she will go." He grinned. "Shall I carry you to the beach, or will you paddle?"

"I can paddle, thanks." She grinned back, rolling her jeans up to knee level. She took off her canvas trainers and threw them on to the sand. In the still hot air, she was conscious of the burning sun on her head and the cool of the water felt delicious on her toes. She longed to swim.

"What about the rest of the stuff?" she enquired, slinging her beach bag over her shoulder.

Mark waded back to the boat and heaved out the picnic and a towel. "We'll collect them when we need them. Let's find a shady spot to leave this lot, and go for a swim."

They chose a large boulder and Anabelle ducked behind it to slip into her plain burgundy swimsuit.

When she stood up, Mark was ready and Anabelle's glance lingered involuntarily on his tall spare frame—angular, yet not boney; well-covered with firm, trained muscle.

"Keep well clear of the rocks. There are a few underwater ones which are sharp and can be dangerous," he said as they strolled to the water's edge.

They splashed in together and Anabelle revelled in the caressing coolness. Her long hair floated freely about her face and she loved the taste of salt on her lips. She swam breastroke for a while, then turned to rest on her back. Her hair fanned out around her. She closed her eyes against the strong sun and listened to the regular splash of Mark's competent freestyle.

There was a tug at her feet. She opened one eye and squinted in the bright light.

"Can you swim under water?" Mark called.

"I don't like it," she replied. "The salt stings my eyes."

"Try it with a mask and snorkel," he suggested. "Come on, we'll get them from the boat."

She followed him lazily and they stood in waist-deep waves to fix their equipment. The mask covered her eyes and nose, and it took a bit of getting used to, but once she realised the advantages, she forgot all the discomfort.

An enchanting underwater world unfolded for her. Tiny fish darted hither and thither amongst the wafting weed. Mark held her hand and led her, pointing out the most interesting rock formations and shellfish.

The time passed rapidly. Anabelle felt the sun grow hot on the back of her neck when they eventually drifted to the shore. They waded wearily through the shallows with their masks pushed high on their foreheads.

"It was beautiful," she enthused. "I had no idea there was so much to see."

"Mmm." Mark nodded in agreement. "It usually is the simple natural things that are, in essence, the most beautiful. And there's much more waiting to be discovered—by those diligent enough to seek it out."

"Do you know this bay well?"

"I used to come here often as a child, but then as I grew up, I came here less frequently. Now, it's my escape from the pressures of business." He smiled suddenly. "It never fails to work."

They had reached the boulder where their things were scattered. Mark stooped to open the cold box. "Drink?" he asked.

"Yes, please."

"Catch." He threw her a can of Coke and Anabelle pressed the cold metal against her hot face.

"Come over here in the shade," he advised. "I think you've had enough sun for one day."

Anabelle agreed and spread out her towel by the rock.

Mark scanned the horizon for a minute, then said, "Do you mind if I leave you alone for a short while?" He pointed to the rocks furthest out to sea. "I want to swim round the edge of the spit over there."

Anabelle followed the line of his outstretched arm. "But that's *miles* away!"

He grinned. "Not really. I'll be wearing flippers. Will you be all right on your own?"

"Of course." She held up the book she was reading. "I've got this." She smiled, opening it at her marked place.

"Fine. I shouldn't be too long." He strode off to the boat to get his flippers.

Anabelle put on her sun-glasses to read,

but found she couldn't concentrate. Her eyes were constantly drawn away from the print to watch Mark as he ploughed steadily through the water, with regular even strokes, towards the rocks.

Anabelle rolled over on her stomach and attempted to read, but it was hopeless and she tossed the book aside in self-disgust.

Restlessly, she sat up and wound her arms around her knees. The horizon pulled her eyes magnetically. She searched the surface of the sea until the glare made them hurt. There was not a single sign of a living soul in or out of the water.

Where was he? she wondered. He could be anywhere, she realised, hidden by the numerous rocks.

She scrambled to her feet and gazed around uncertainly. There should be *some* indication of his whereabouts. She walked down to the shoreline feeling helpless, and idly paddled about. And all the time she scanned the waves for some sign of life.

She became annoyed with herself for being so susceptible to his welfare. But she *was* concerned and she couldn't stop herself. Then suddenly he was there and her heart was beating fast in relief and anger at the same time. His dark head was riding just above the waves. He was swimming slowly, on his back or on his side, she thought. She started, then splashed forward, knee-deep into the water, alarmed that he may have been injured by some underwater hazard.

"Mark! Hi, there!" she called, and waved.

His head jerked up at the sound of her voice. He stopped swimming and trod water for a moment to wave back.

Of course he was all right! Anabelle laughed at her worry and felt foolish. Then a sudden burst of insight exploded in her head, taking her by surprise. She frowned. She couldn't, could she? Could she be falling in love with him? Would that explain her feelings?

He was nearer now. She waded further into the sea until it reached her waist. Mark swam towards her. He stopped a few yards distant and stood upright while he removed his flippers and tucked them under his arm.

His black unruly hair was now plastered, seal-like, to his head. It curled at the nape of his neck, to his smooth, tanned shoulders. Seawater ran in rivulets down his lean body making his skin glisten in the bright light. She wanted him. Her body ached for him.

"Enjoying yourself?" he asked with a smile.

"Y-Yes. Yes, thanks," she stammered.

"Is anything wrong?"

"No." She shrugged as if by way of explanation, then added, "You were gone for rather a long time."

"Was I? I'm sorry. I didn't mean to alarm you."

He looked down at her and laughed. His easy, relaxed attitude attracted her as much as his vibrant masculine presence. He drew her like a magnet, a powerful magnet.

For a moment their eyes met and held with an unspoken message that they both understood. She saw in his face desire; desire for her, and a tingle spread throughout her body and limbs. She felt the same for him and it showed. She knew it showed.

She thought he would kiss her, but he didn't. He tapped her lightly on her nose and said, "Your skin's beginning to burn. Come over to the shade."

It was lunchtime and they were hungry. Mark unpacked the picnic that he'd put together himself. He'd made huge sandwiches from sections of French loaves. The meat and salad fillings spilled out into their foil wrappings. He pulled the ring-tabs from a couple of cans of lager and they both leaned against the boulder to drink from the cans.

Anabelle closed her eyes, contented, and sighed.

"Happy?" Mark asked casually.

"Mmm," she replied, non-comittally.

There was a lengthy silence. Then she heard him move. She felt his fingers in her hair and she held her breath.

"Just a few small stones caught in your hair," he explained.

He knocked them away carefully, then, as he removed his hand, he drew it smoothly down her neck and across the line of her shoulder.

"Such beautiful skin," he said softly.

She opened her eyes a fraction. He was very close to her, leaning full stretch, on one elbow, and watching her steadily. As his hand slowly began to massage the curve of her shoulder, her desire became so strong that she thought she would cry out. Her eyes opened fully and, as he leaned further towards her, she didn't resist as he lowered his mouth to hers. Tenderly, he explored her lips, her eyes, her throat. Her heart thudded loudly, evenly, in her ears. She wanted to be near him and her body melted under his touch.

He kissed her temples and her hair, and she shivered involuntarily. For a second he was still. Very still. And then she moved, just one tiny movement towards him. But it was enough and their bodies were in contact as if they always should have been.

He kissed her with such a wild, unleashed sensuality that her head reeled. She glimpsed the hungry flare in his eyes. and, for a tantalising second, thought she should tear herself away from him and run. But it was already too late. His lips and hands were expertly seducing any resistance away from her.

She locked her arms around his neck, wanting him closer. His kisses deepened and lengthened, and her fingers laced through his hair, clinging tightly as if she were holding on to the last vestiges of life itself.

She found it exciting and vaguely frightening at the same time. His mouth and hands and body were showing her, very clearly, how much he wanted her and her own body was responding outside of her control; yearning for him, every one of her movements telling him so.

But her head said no, she must resist him. Yet, how could she, when her body continued to say yes? He would make love to her, she knew. Unless she stopped him now. A grain of sanity remained. She must act now, before it was too late.

She tore herself away from him and cried, "No. No more. Please no more. We must stop."

She could feel the tense, throbbing passion inside him, and his voice was ragged in his throat. "You can't stop now, Anabelle. You want me. I know you do."

She moved her head from side to side to deny his words.

His arms tightened about her again. "Don't lie, Anabelle," he breathed.

His mouth sought the velvet of her neck

and he kissed her along her shoulder until she could no longer bear it.

She pushed at him with all her strength and tried to wriggle free. "No. I—I can't," she cried. "It's—It's—" She choked on the words, silenced by his angry face as he held her firmly, beneath him. "I can't go on," she repeated in a whisper. "I—I'm sorry."

"Sorry!" He moved away from her and jack-knifed into a sitting position, his back towards her. His voice was hoarse and he sounded bitter. "It's a bit late to be sorry now! Why on earth didn't you stop me earlier? Is this your idea of a game?"

"No," she whispered, full of remorse. "I've said I'm sorry."

"You deliberately led me on!" he accused.

No! It wasn't true! She didn't mean to. It just happened. She lost control. Oh dear, what had she done?

He ran his hands furiously through his hair. "Haven't you learned yet that you shouldn't start things you have no intention of finishing?"

"I didn't start it," she said quietly.

He turned on her, his green eyes flashing, full of wrath.

"You gave me all the signs," he seethed. "Don't deny it! You knew damn well what you were doing—and what it would lead to!"

Yes, she acquiesced silently. But total commitment wasn't a step she could take that easily. She needed an emotional commitment before she could enter into a physical relationship.

She loved him, of that she was now sure. But what of him? Did he love her? She thought not. He would take what was offered—if she was willing—and probably move on. And then she would feel used and cheap.

Yes, he was right. She wanted him. If she was going to survive with her self-respect intact, she'd better stay well away from him in future. She wouldn't let it happen again. Ever.

"Women!" She heard him mutter a curse.

"It wasn't deliberate," she insisted quietly.

"Forget it, eh?" he snapped. He exhaled

audibly and his shoulders sagged. "I'm going for a swim."

The afternoon was spoiled. When he returned from his long and energetic swim, he was offhand with her; polite but nothing more as they gathered together their things to pack the boat.

Anabelle was subdued; drained by the self-revelation of her behaviour. She had never felt like this with any other man. But then, she had never been with any man quite like Mark Dalgetti. She couldn't relax and forget the incident, as he suggested. She shrugged mentally. Maybe he could, if she was just another girl to him.

An indefinable tension sprang between them which affected their communication. They were stiff and formal with each other. It seemed as if they could no longer touch or talk in a casual manner, and the journey back in *Alison* was awkward.

The joy of the fresh salt air was gone. They motored slowly, through a calm sea under a baking sun. Anabelle sat hunched in the front, hard against the side, trailing her hand idly in the water and trying to ignore Mark's presence beside her. It was an impossible task. He was too real, too alive, too close, too—her head jerked up to look at him as she searched for the words. He was staring at her; his intense green eyes more brilliant now in contrast with his tan, penetrating her innermost uncertainties.

"Your back's red," he said shortly. "Here, put this on."

He reached over to the rear seat and shook out his shirt. She accepied it gratefully. Ali had said he was an understanding and considerate man. It was true. she thought. Sometimes. She wondered how long Ali had worked for Mark. Ali. *Alison*. Had he named the boat after her? If he had they must be pretty close. Lovers? She couldn't bear to think about it.

They reached the villa, tired and thirsty. Anabelle flopped into a chair on the terrace.

"I desperately need a drink," Mark stated flatly. "Do you want to shower?"

She did, but she refused. "I'd rather get back to the hotel," she replied, standing up. "I want to ring my mother before it gets too late."

"Still intent on running home to Mummy?"

Anabelle flushed and remained silent. She just wanted to talk to her, to hear her mother's side of the story. She would then try to restore her own equilibrium—if she could.

Mark was walking into the lounge through the French doors.

"Phone her from here while I make some tea." He shrugged. "I don't feel like driving just at the moment." He strode over to the telephone and picked up the receiver. "I'll get the number for you," he added, flicking over the pages of his telephone index. "Which one? Shop or flat?"

"I—I—" Anabelle had to stop and think what day it was, and what time. "Oh —er—the shop, I expect," she conceded.

It was good to hear Joanna's voice. The line was surprisingly clear and they chattered excitedly for a few minutes until Joanna tentatively asked about Rupert and Eleanor. Hesitating, Anabelle related the events of their first meeting—her grandfather's illness and sudden relapse and, particularly, Eleanor's frosty reception. Finally, Anabelle took a deep breath and voiced her qualms.

"Mother." She paused. "They say you were responsible for Father's death."

There was a long silence at the other end of the line.

8

"MOTHER? Are you still there?"

"Yes, darling." Another silence. Anabelle heard her mother sigh. "I thought after all these years they might have found it in their hearts to forgive."

"You mean it's true?"

"No. Not at all. Your grandfather believed it at the time of the accident. It was the main reason he wanted to take you away from me. I assumed with this attempt at reconciliation that Eleanor must have told him what really happened. She was there, with us, when we crashed."

"She says you killed him."

"She's lying!" Joanna sounded annoyed. "My goodness, she hasn't changed much, has she?"

"Mother, why didn't you tell me about all this? Why didn't you warn me?"

"I didn't want to poison your mind against them any more than I had done already. Eleanor was in the car with your father and me. She was concussed—as I was—and always maintained she could remember nothing of the accident. Personally, I never really believed her. I thought that, maybe, after all this time, she had regrets and would tell the truth."

"What is the truth, Mum?" Anabelle interrupted.

Joanna sounded weary. "You ought to know, I suppose. The truth is—Paul was drunk. We all were. We'd been to a party and there were a lot of people who'd seen us drinking steadily—and said so afterwards. Eleanor was there, too. She used to get so distraught about things sometimes. She'd had a row with some man and, well, in the end she persuaded us to drive her home." She sighed heavily. "We came off a bend and hit a lamp-post. The driver's door flew open and your father was thrown out."

"Father was driving?"

"Yes. He'd swerved to avoid a stray dog and lost control. I was in the front passenger seat and my door had jammed. I'd hit my head, but all I could think about was getting out to Paul. I crawled across the driver's seat and—and I must have blacked out over the wheel."

"And everyone believed you were driving?"

"Yes."

"But why didn't you deny it, Mother?"

"For Paul's sake, darling. He was having enough trouble from his father already. And Rupert thought the worst of me anyway, so I had nothing to lose except —except—"

"Oh, Mum," Anabelle choked.

"They didn't tell me he was dead. I was in hospital and they didn't tell me until I'd recovered. I couldn't deny it then, could I?"

"What did Eleanor say?"

"Nothing. She had concussion and nobody put any pressure on her. There were no witnesses." Joanna hesitated. "She never really liked me. She always sided with her father."

As they talked it became clear to Anabelle how her grandfather's attitude to her mother had cemented. The accident must have been the final straw for him. He blamed Joanna for his only son's alienation and it was not in his nature to forgive her for causing his death. His reaction had been to remove Joanna's influence from his son's child. Or, at least, to have tried to.

When she rang off, Anabelle had not mentioned going home.

She replaced the receiver and sat staring into space, reflecting on her change of mind. Her grandfather was wrong, she thought fiercely. Suddenly, it became very important to her to put the record straight. Her mother may have been prepared to let her grandfather go on believing lies, but she wasn't. She must talk frankly to him before she left; and that would mean waiting until he was well enough to see her again. She resolved not to leave the island until this misunderstanding had been sorted out.

"Anabelle?"

She started, roused abruptly from her thoughts. "Sorry, did you say something? I was miles away."

"Obviously," Mark replied drily. He was standing beside her with a glass of lemon tea in a silver filigree holder.

"Well? When do you leave?" he demanded shortly.

"I'm not," she stated. "I'm staying."

Immediately, he looked puzzled, but she didn't enlighten him. She took pleasure in seeing him thrown off balance for a moment and added sweetly, "You win."

He frowned. He wasn't sure whether or not she meant it and she was glad. Let him think what he likes! she thought. He's probably arrogant enough to think my decision has something to do with him! If he does, he's in for a big surprise.

The frown persisted as they drank their tea and he drove her back to the hotel. He switched off the engine and sat in silence, staring out of the windscreen.

Anabelle leaned on the door handle and said, with a forced cheeriness. "Thanks for a lovely day, then."

He stretched across and stilled her progress, covering her hand with his.

She caught her breath and her pulse thudded.

"If you've really decided to stay, perhaps we can repeat it," he suggested.

"No, thank you," she responded stiffly.

"Oh, come on, Anabelle, there's no need to sulk. This is a beautiful island.

I'll take you round it and show you the sights."

"I can make my own arrangements, Mark."

He removed his hand pointedly and shrugged. "OK. I recognise a brush-off when I hear one." He sat back in his seat and looked straight ahead. His face was grim and his voice was hard. "Goodbye, Anabelle."

"Goodbye, Mark."

She scrambled out of the car and walked quickly into the hotel. her heart thumping in her throat. She did not allow herself a backward glance.

After a shower, she felt better; fresh and cool in a blue and white cotton skirt and top. She was brushing her hair and wondering how her grandfather was when there was a knock on her door. It was Eleanor. Anabelle knew she would have to make her peace with her aunt.

"Please come in," she said. "Sit down."

Eleanor's eyes travelled round the room, resting on the untidy heap of beach clothes that Anabelle hadn't yet removed.

"Had a good day?" the older woman queried.

"We went swimming. Mark told me my grandfather wouldn't be allowed to see me until he was better."

"Mark was just protecting his own interests!" Eleanor retaliated sharply.

Anabelle replaced her hairbrush carefully on the dressing-table. "How is my grandfather this evening?" she said quietly.

"Slightly improved. He wants to see you, but you can't stay long."

Eleanor took Anabelle to their suite of rooms on the north side of the hotel. The sitting-room was spacious and shady, with louvred shutters closed against the bright Mediterranean light. It was plainly furnished. The overwhelming feature was the collection of paintings hanging round the walls—her father's paintings. Anabelle's head turned from side to side in wonder as Eleanor led her through the room to the adjoining bedroom.

Rupert was sitting up in bed looking frail in white pyjamas and white sheets. Just inside the door, Anabelie saw a small easel carrying the portrait of Joanna.

It was a good likeness. Simple, almost

ethereal in atmosphere, not futuristically stylised as many of her father's other paintings were. She hadn't seen it since the auction, and, confronted with it again, she wanted it more now than she did then.

Rupert dismissed her sympathies and pleasantries with an impatient gesture. "They're sending me to the mainland for treatment. To Rome. Before I leave I want to give you this." He pointed to the portrait. "It's yours, Anabelle. As I promised."

Anabelle glanced at Eleanor and wondered if her grandfather knew of their conversation that morning. Her aunt's face was unreadable, though her eyes glittered and her mouth was pinched.

In those few seconds of silence, Rupert added, "It's a belated coming-of-age present, my dear."

"Thank you, Grandfather," Anabelle said sincerely.

His tired wrinkled features didn't alter. He gave a nod and addressed his daughter. "Eleanor, go and arrange for it to be hung in Anabelle's room." He dismissed her as he would a servant, but, strangely, Anabelle thought, she didn't seem to mind. "Come and sit down, child," he went on, turning to Anabelle.

She drew a chair to the bedside and sat down dutifully.

"What do you think of Mark Dalgetti?" Rupert asked.

Floored, Anabelle was momentarily speechless. She shrugged and grimaced. "He's all right, I suppose," she said with mock indifference. "He seems to know where he's going."

"He does indeed. He's a shrewd fellow and a very astute businessman. So was his father. I respect his judgment, and he tells me that, as well as being attractive, you have an intelligent head on your shoulders."

In spite of! he probably meant, Anabelle thought, her irritation mounting. Why did everything always have to come round to Mark? Why couldn't she get away from him?

"I've been brought up to run a business," she explained. "It's small but it's had its problems." She lifted her chin a fraction. "My mother gave me very good training. I owe it all to her."

"And your Cavendish blood! She owed

231

you! Your mother had a lot to make up to you considering what you might have had! But no! She took you away—and my son," he finished bitterly.

"She wasn't driving! She didn't kill him!"

Oh dear! She hadn't meant to tell him now. She'd meant to wait until he was stronger. She pushed her hair back from her face and stood up. "I'm sorry, Grandfather. I don't want to upset you. I'd better go."

"No. Stay. Sit down. Get me a glass of water."

Anabelle did as he asked and he swallowed a couple of pills. When he was calmer, she sat down again.

"Your mother told you this, I suppose?" Rupert enquired.

"It's the truth, Grandfather. Ask Aunt Eleanor. She was there in the car."

"She says she doesn't remember."

"That's convenient for her," Anabelle returned quietly. There was an uneasy silence between them. Then she went on, "That was rude, I'm sorry. But my mother wouldn't lie."

"And my daughter isn't without her faults, I know. I'll talk to her before I leave for Rome."

"When are you going?"

"When I'm strong enough to make the journey." Her grandfather held out his gnarled fingers. "Stay, my dear. Stay and come and see me every day. We've a lot of lost time to make up."

She took his ice-cold hand in hers and nodded. "I'll stay, Grandfather," she said.

Over the next few days, she visited her grandfather for half-an-hour each evening. He liked her to read to him. Occasionally, he was playing chess with an acquaintance and she was excused.

One afternoon, Anabelle decided to take the local bus to Ischia Porto, the main port on the island. The harbour was almost perfectly round for, at one time, it had been the crater of a volcano.

Anabelle found the town enchanting. It was full of narrow streets that frequently turned into flights of steps, and flat-roofed, vaguely oriental-looking houses which climbed steeply up a hillside topped by pine trees.

Local fishing-boats jostled with

expensive pleasure craft, and boutiques. Pottery shops and cafés lined the harbour with life and colour. By lunchtime the air was filled with the delicious aromas of freshly cooked pizza and charcoal grilled fish. Anabelle chose a pavement café, and a table under its awning to give her a good view of the harbour. With some help from the waitress, who was a student, she ordered fresh anchovies and, while waiting for them to arrive, she began to write some postcards.

She was chewing her pen and staring into space when a familiar flame-red flying-suit distracted her attention. Ali! Here? A crowd of boisterous teenagers passed in front of her and when they'd gone, Anabelle saw who Ali was with. She had her arm linked in Mark's and they were talking, joking and laughing as they strode together along the quayside. They didn't see her and Anabelle didn't call to them. They looked so happy, Anabelle thought. Her heart turned to a piece of cold stone and sank down to her feet.

She finished her meal, then wandered round the harbour. *Dalgetti III* wasn't there. Was it still in Naples? she wondered. If so, what was Ali doing here? What indeed! Mark wasn't the sort of man to go around without a girl on his arm. She shrugged. Oh, well, she'd had her chance and walked away. But that didn't prevent her from wanting him still. And loving him.

Irritatingly, she couldn't get him out of her mind. Despite all her efforts to concentrate on the shops and the sights, her thoughts returned constantly to him. His image was so strong that half the time she imagined she saw him in the distance, only to find, on second glance, she was wrong.

She didn't see him again that afternoon. Annoyed with the effect the chance sighting had on her, she caught an early bus back to the hotel. The beautiful scenery was wasted on her. She spent the journey reliving moments with him; good, bad, happy, sad. They were all, she realised, memories. Just memories.

A good hot soak, some heated rollers in her hair, her pretty, sugared-almond check dress, and Anabelle felt better. But when she went along to see her grandfather at the customary time, she was taken aback to see Mark in the sitting-room with Rupert, playing chess.

"Grandfather!" she exclaimed spontaneously. "You're well enough to get up!"

Rupert nodded. "I'm leaving for Rome tomorrow." He was seated at the chess-table wearing a loose linen suit, and studying the chess-pieces. Mark, too, wore a suit; lightweight and light grey, with a white shirt and dark grey tie. It was such a surprising change from the casual jeans he'd worn earlier with Ali. The atmosphere seemed formal to Anabelle and she hesitated, wondering if she should leave them to their game.

"Hello, Anabelle." Mark stood up to greet her. He smiled.

"Good evening, Mark," she replied politely. "Am I interrupting anything?"

"No, my dear. Sit down." It was Rupert who answered her. "Eleanor will be joining us shortly." Her grandfather straightened up from the board. "I've talked to her. About—about Paul's accident." He paused. "My judgment of Joanna may have been hasty. However—"

he shrugged—"it's not too late to make amends. I've written to your mother, my dear, and asked her to visit me. Do you think she will?"

Anabelle chewed her lip. "I don't know."

Mark moved towards her and said, "You can persuade her, Anabelle. If you want to." His green eyes were narrowed, as though challenging her to refuse.

She sat down hastily. "I'll try." Privately she thought Joanna would now see her father-in-law. The misunderstanding could be cleared completely, the olive branch accepted. Joanna wouldn't need persuading.

"Thank you." Rupert nodded. "Bring your chair closer. We have to talk."

"I'll be in the bar if you want me, sir," Mark interjected.

"No, stay. You are as good as family, Mark. I have no financial secrets from you." Her grandfather was quite firm, and Mark returned to his chair. Rupert continued. "I plan to see my lawyers in Rome and change my Will. There is no hurry, of course." He tapped his chest with a clenched fist. "I've got a few years yet."

He was interrupted as Eleanor joined them, looking dramatic in a gold and black evening trouser-suit. She gave Anabelle a weak smile before settling elegantly in a comfortable armchair.

Rupert went on. "There are not many changes and they are my wishes. Eleanor knows of them—and approves. Paul's paintings will be yours, Anabelle. All of them. Eleanor will have my property in England, and the income from it, until she dies. But only in trust. Then it passes to you, Anabelle, and after you, your children. Meanwhile, my dear, you will have my investment stock. I have shares in one or two successful business ventures and they should give you a regular return. I have confidence you'll use them wisely."

"Thank you, Grandfather." Anabelle stole a glance at Eleanor.

The older woman smiled back weakly again. She appeared to be satisfied with her father's decisions.

"Splendid. But there remains one problem." Rupert frowned for a second. "Eleanor is accompanying me to Rome which means Anabelle will be left on her own in the hotel."

Anabelle grimaced. She didn't relish the idea of staying alone in any hotel. And there weren't many people of her own age in this one.

"Could I come with you?" she suggested.

"I prefer not," her grandfather replied, looking at Eleanor.

Anabelle lifted her shoulders non-chalantly. "Don't worry about me. I'll be quite all right, I'm sure."

"You could stay with me at the villa," Mark volunteered casually. He had been quiet until then and Anabelle's reaction was to refuse immediately. But she didn't get the opportunity.

"Excellent idea!" Rupert agreed, nodding at Mark. "You'll take good care of her, m'boy, won't you?"

"Very good care," Mark replied seriously.

"But I—" Anabelle began.

"An ideal solution," her grandfather interrupted. "I've been concerned about leaving you."

"Then let me relieve you of the worry."
Mark smiled.

"Indeed I shall," Rupert responded.
"You have no objections, have you,
Anabelle?"

She could think of nothing to say, or at
least, no reason she felt able to disclose to
her grandfather. Her voice sounded un-
naturally high as she said, "Er—er—no.
None."

"Fine." Rupert seemed very pleased. "I
shall rest much easier knowing you are
well looked after by Mark."

"Come with me now, Anabelle," Mark
said. "We can have dinner together on the
way to the villa."

"Now?" Anabelle echoed faintly. "I
can't." she argued feebly, "I'm not
packed."

"Nonsense, my dear," Rupert interjected. "Run along and collect a few over-
night things. The hotel will send on
anything else you need."

Mark smiled at her. "I'll wait for you in
the foyer, Anabelle."

Initially annoyed at the way the arrangements had been made for her, she had
composed herself by the time she walked

out of her room to go down to the foyer. Mark and she were, after all, both adults. Surely they could respect each other's views and behave in a reasonable, rational way for a few days?

As Anabelle approached the lift, she saw Eleanor, waiting for her. A slight smile played about the older woman's mouth.

"Well," Eleanor said. "I hope you're satisfied with your booty. I know it's not as much as you'd planned but—"

"Please, Aunt Eleanor. I didn't *plan* for any of it. Can't we be friends, at last?"

"Huh. You'll need a friend if you take up with Mark Dalgetti. You know why he's so interested in you, don't you? It's those shares you'll get. They're all shares in Mark's companies. That's the attraction you have for him. I thought you ought to know. He's only protecting his own interests."

The lift came and Anabelle stepped inside. She tried to remain pleasant. She managed a stiff smile. "I see. Thank you for the warning, Aunt. Please let me know how my grandfather progresses." She pressed the button and the doors slid shut.

She supposed Eleanor was telling the truth. It made sense of the connection between Mark and Rupert Cavendish. She'd suspected from the beginning that Rupert had some kind of lever on Mark. This was it. And now he was giving it to her. But she didn't want it. She didn't want Mark's attention for her shares.

He was, certainly, very charming when she joined him in the hotel foyer. She had been on the receiving end of his charm before—when he wanted something. He drove her to a rustic pizzeria in the hills. It was very atmospheric; checked cloths, flickering candlelight and a plaintive guitar player strumming melancholy tunes. The pizza was enormous; a cartwheel in size and shape, with different flavoured toppings radiating from the centre. The wine they had with it was a good local wine.

Mark told her that *Dalgetti III* was moving on to the Costa Smeralda in Sardinia and that she was a great success. Anabelle voiced her pleasure at this news.

They'd finished the pizza and Mark,

leaning back, said: "I didn't think you'd come with me."

"I could hardly refuse without upsetting Grandfather and I do want to see him well again."

"Is that the only reason?"

"Yes. Should there be another? What's *your* reason for offering me a bed. You're no knight in shining armour."

"True," he agreed readily. "You know my reason. I want to make love to you."

"And, of course," she retaliated, "you're interested in my shares!"

He crashed his fist down on to the cloth. His green eyes flashed angrily. "My goodness! You can be cynical at times!"

"But you don't deny it! They are shares in your companies!"

"Yes."

"Well then?"

"Well then!" he repeated sarcastically. "Finish your wine, Anabelle, and I'll take you home. You certainly know how to put a man off, don't you?" He leaned across the table and lowered his voice ominously. "For your information, lady, those shares were originally left to me. I persuaded your grandfather to give them to you. I thought they were your birthright. But, if you don't want to soil your pretty little hands with commerce, I can buy them from you. Twice over if I have to. I'm not exactly destitute."

"I—I—" she inhaled deeply. "There's really no need to get so angry—"

"Isn't there?" he snapped. He stood up, not waiting for her to finish her wine. "Come on. Let's go. It's late."

He drove to the villa impatiently, accelerating too fast on the straight and braking too sharply on the bends. He curtly offered to make coffee, but Anabelle refused. She wanted to escape from the brusque treatment she was receiving as soon as possible.

Mark showed her the bathroom and her bedroom, then left her standing in the open doorway and went downstairs. It was a hot, stifling night and there was no air-conditioning. She kicked off her shoes and walked barefoot on the cold ceramic tiled floor. The wine was making her drowsy and her head was beginning to ache. She washed quickly and undressed, flinging herself into bed and praying for the oblivion of sleep.

Her prayer was answered, but it was short-lived. She awoke about three hours later, feeling hot and thirsty. It was dark and the moonlight shone into her open window casting blue shadows on the walls. Her thirst got worse. It must have been the pizza or the wine. Probably both. She would have to get up for a drink.

As she went down to the kitchen, she noticed a light on in the dining-room. The door was slightly ajar. She stopped outside and listened. All was silent. She crept into the kitchen and took a bottle of cold mineral water from the fridge. It tasted like nectar from heaven and she felt better immediately.

There was no one else about, she decided. The dining-room light must have been left on by mistake. She stole in to switch it off on her way back.

She stopped in her tracks. Mark was in there. Asleep. It looked as though he had been reading at ihe dining-table and had fallen asleep over the books. He was slumped forward, his head resting on his arms. His jacket was tossed on a nearby chair and crumpled in a heap. The reading lamp cast a mellow pool of light over broad shoulders, motionless in sleep.

Should she turn it out? She padded quietly across the tiles. Her fingers were halfway to the switch when she stopped. She stood stock-still and stared at him. His shirt stretched taut across his back, the seams straining against the firm, developed muscle. His unruly black hair curled, too long, over his collar.

Anabelle's hand hovered in mid-air. Inexplicably, it was drawn towards him. She held it, a couple of inches away and traced the shape of his strong arms and shoulders. The desire to caress him was almost too powerful for her.

"I love him," she whispered. "I love him with all my heart and with all my soul, and I want him to love me too."

She switched off the light with a soft click and moved silently to the door. She heard a movement as she reached it.

"Who's there? Who is it?"

She could slip out quietly and pretend she hadn't heard him. Yes, that would be the best thing to do, the most sensible.

"Anabelle? Is that you?"

She heard the chair creak.

"Don't go, Anabelle. I want to talk to you."

"No," she croaked. "I can't stay. I daren't," she thought.

She ran. She ran out of the dining-room and up to the sanctuary of her bedroom.

Such a short burst of exercise shouldn't have made her out of breath. But her chest was rising and falling rapidly, and her heart was thumping in her ears as she leaned on the closed door.

"I love him," she whispered to her reflection in the mirror. "I want him. More than anything, I want him."

"Anabelle!" Mark's voice was urgent. "May I come in?"

She whirled away from the door as though it were red hot. The word "no" froze on her lips. She couldn't refuse him. She knew she couldn't.

Then he was standing in front of her, the collar of his shirt unbuttoned and his hands shoved carelessly into the pockets of his trousers.

"We can't ignore this, Anabelle," he said. "Not any more." Slowly, he lifted his arms and reached towards her. "Come here, Anabelle. Come here to me."

It was as if he had thrown silken threads around her and pulled on them. They tightened and she found herself moving, trance-like into his arms. She had run from him in the dining-room, but she couldn't run from him now. Her hands rose, automatically, to connect with his. Strong, lean fingers entwined in hers, then gripped them with a ferocity that surprised her.

She was jerked towards him and his lean features were uncompromisingly hard with desire in the silver moonlight.

She wanted him to want her, to love her, and she did not resist when his sensuous mouth came down on hers, inflaming her passion even more.

She returned his kisses, unashamedly, as he continued to kiss her eyes, hair and neck, returning, searingly, to her lips.

She was vaguely aware of the bed behind her knees and, as he pushed her gently backwards, she found she was lying on the bed.

In seconds he was beside her, caressing her, coaxing her into a willing surrender.

How expert he was at loving! Loving? No. This wasn't love for him. She mustn't kid herself. Her yielding body stiffened as she hesitated. And he noticed. He paused.

"What's wrong, Anabelle?" he murmured.

"N-nothing. I—I'm not very experienced, that's all."

She thought she saw him smile. He held her close and kissed her as though to reassure her. But it didn't. He *was* experienced and she wasn't, and the thought of his experiences hurt. Had Ali stayed here last night? In this bed? With Mark? The idea tortured her and it showed.

"You're tense, Anabelle. You must relax."

"I'm s-sorry," she stammered.

"You're frowning. What's wrong?" he asked again.

She was trembling, she knew. She shook her head.

He moved away from her. "You're supposed to be enjoying this," he said quietly.

"I—I *am*," she insisted.

"Come off it! You look as though you despise me. Do you?"

"No! Truly, I don't want you to stop."

"And in the morning you'll hate me!" he retaliated. "That's not what *I* want, Anabelle!" He sat up.

"Mark, please, don't go!"

He was already on his feet. "Where you're concerned, I don't know what I do want. I wish to hell I'd never set eyes on you, Anabelle Todd!"

He strode aggressively from her room.

It was a long time before she slept. She wept until, at last, exhausted, she drifted off to sleep.

She woke early, feeling drained and feverish from lack of sleep. Her composure was shattered, her emotions confused. She couldn't face him yet. Not just yet.

Very quietly, she dressed in shorts and T-shirt and crept out of the villa, down the stone steps to the pool. The sun was already dazzlingly bright, and the air hot and still. She sat on the edge of the tiles and dangled her bare toes in the cool water. The oleanders were in blossom, their frilly rose-pink blooms enlivening the greenery that surrounded the villa and the pool.

"I wish I didn't love him so much. If I didn't, it wouldn't hurt so much." Such futile thoughts were no solution, she realised dejectedly.

She heard the French doors slide open and her head jerked upwards. Mark stood on the terrace and stared down at her. He wore a *Dalgetti III* T-shirt and his old jeans. He leaned on the stone parapet and watched her silently for a moment. She looked away.

"Can we talk?" he called softly.

"If you want to." She gazed at the water, shimmering in the early morning sun.

"I want to," he replied. "Do you?"

"I've nothing to say," she thought, "except 'I love you' and that's probably better left unsaid."

"Do you?" he repeated, louder.

She shrugged. "I don't mind."

He walked slowly down the stone steps. As he came closer, she saw how drawn and tired he was. Dark shadows circled his eyes.

"I didn't sleep well," he said.

"Neither did I."

He stopped beside her, stooped, and

hooked a finger under her chin. "Yes," he agreed. "You look tired."

"So do you."

"We can't go on like this."

"No. Why did you walk out on me?"

"I don't know exactly, Anabelle. It was the expression on your face, in your eyes, as if you were frightened of something—of me perhaps."

"I wasn't."

"I thought you were. I didn't want to hurt you. I couldn't bear to think you might despise me for what I did to you." He squatted on his haunches by her side. "I've never felt like this before about any woman." His eyes searched hers as he continued. "Anabelle, I'm in love with you."

A tingle of pleasure spread through the whole of her body. Her eyes shone with unshed tears. "Oh, Mark," she choked, "I've loved you since—since—the day on the beach."

"You what?" he whispered in disbelief. "But you gave me the brush-off! You sent me away! Why? In heaven's name, why?"

"I didn't want to get hurt. I knew you wanted to make love to me and I knew I wouldn't be able to say no to you. You hadn't said you loved me and I didn't know if there was anyone else . . ."

"Anyone else?"

She shrugged. "You seemed to get on so well with Ali. I saw you together yesterday in Ischia Porto and—and there's the boat named after her."

"Which boat?"

"Your powerboat *Alison*."

His features twisted in exasperation. "You silly goose! Alison is my mother. Ali's name is Natalie."

"Oh." She did feel a fool.

He laughed gently. "I knew Ali had designs on me. I liked her well enough and she was an excellent worker. But she wanted more out of the arrangement than I did, so I paid her off in the nicest possible way. She understood, and we parted friends. She's gone to Venice to work for a tour operator."

"Oh. I see."

"Darling Anabelle, there is no one else, I promise you."

"Mark, I love you so much I—" The tears spilled over and her words were lost.

"Hey, come here." Mark stood up and

drew her to her feet. "It took me a while to work out what was happening to me. But when I realised how much you meant to me, how important your feelings were to me, I knew I was in love with you. And as soon as I knew, I had to tell you." He kissed her lightly on the tip of her nose. "But, if I'd known you were going to cry, I'd have kept it to myself." There was a twinkle in his eye and a crooked grin on his lips. "I thought you'd be happy," he said in mock surprise.

She sniffed and grinned back. "I am. Oh, I am."

"Are you sure?" he asked solicitously. He was teasing her, she realised. She guessed she deserved it. "I don't want to marry you if it makes you sad," he added.

"Marry me?" she queried faintly.

"People in love get married, don't they?"

"Yes," she agreed, wiping away the tears with the back of her hand.

"Well? When do we?"

"Do we what?"

"Get married, idiot," he continued patiently.

"You don't waste much time, do you?"
"No," he replied firmly.
And he didn't.

THE END

GUIDE
TO THE COLOUR CODING
OF
ULVERSCROFT BOOKS

Many of our readers have written to us expressing their appreciation for the way in which our colour coding has assisted them in selecting the Ulverscroft books of their choice. To remind everyone of our colour coding— this is as follows:

BLACK COVERS
Mysteries

*

BLUE COVERS
Romances

*

RED COVERS
Adventure Suspense and General Fiction

*

ORANGE COVERS
Westerns

*

GREEN COVERS
Non-Fiction

ROMANCE TITLES
in the
Ulverscroft Large Print Series

THE SHADOWS
OF THE CROWN TITLES
in the
Ulverscroft Large Print Series

The Tudor Rose   *Margaret Campbell Barnes*
Brief Gaudy Hour *Margaret Campbell Barnes*
Mistress Jane Seymour   *Frances B. Clark*
My Lady of Cleves

Margaret Campbell Barnes
Katheryn The Wanton Queen

Maureen Peters
The Sixth Wife   *Jean Plaidy*
The Last Tudor King   *Hester Chapman*
Young Bess   *Margaret Irwin*
Lady Jane Grey   *Hester Chapman*
Elizabeth, Captive Princess   *Margaret Irwin*
Elizabeth and The Prince of Spain

Margaret Irwin
Gay Lord Robert   *Jean Plaidy*
Here Was A Man   *Norah Lofts*
Mary Queen of Scotland:
The Triumphant Year   *Jean Plaidy*
The Captive Queen of Scots   *Jean Plaidy*
The Murder in the Tower   *Jean Plaidy*
The Young and Lonely King   *Jane Lane*
King's Adversary   *Monica Beardsworth*
A Call of Trumpets   *Jane Lane*

FICTION TITLES
in the
Ulverscroft Large Print Series

The Onedin Line: The High Seas
                              Cyril Abraham
The Onedin Line: The Iron Ships
                              Cyril Abraham
The Onedin Line: The Shipmaster
                              Cyril Abraham
The Onedin Line: The Trade Winds
                              Cyril Abraham
The Enemy   *Desmond Bagley*
Flyaway   *Desmond Bagley*
The Master Idol   *Anthony Burton*
The Navigators   *Anthony Burton*
A Place to Stand   *Anthony Burton*
The Doomsday Carrier   *Victor Canning*
The Cinder Path   *Catherine Cookson*
The Girl   *Catherine Cookson*
The Invisible Cord   *Catherine Cookson*
Life and Mary Ann   *Catherine Cookson*
Maggie Rowan   *Catherine Cookson*
Marriage and Mary Ann   *Catherine Cookson*
Mary Ann's Angels   *Catherine Cookson*
All Over the Town   *R. F. Delderfield*
Jamaica Inn   *Daphne du Maurier*
My Cousin Rachel   *Daphne du Maurier*

NON-FICTION TITLES
in the
Ulverscroft Large Print Series